SERENA BLANDISH

or

The Difficulty of Getting Married

by

A LADY of QVALITY , pseud.

[Enid Bagnold]

The Suicide

Lady of Q.

GEORGE H. DORAN COMPANY
On Murray Hill · · · · New York

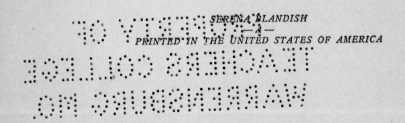

SERENA BLANDISH

SERENA BLANDISH

or

The Difficulty of Getting Married

CHAPTER I

AMONG all the women who lived in a garden city adjoining the southern docks of London, none was so charming or so uncommon as Miss Serena Blandish, a young girl of nineteen to whom Nature had given every grace of figure, face, ankle, wrist, and expression.

Gentle and docile with her family, she was at first almost silent with strangers, shy at parties, fêtes, and dances, where sitting modestly with her head a little bent forward and her eyes from time to time stealing upwards and as quickly dropping, she would attract everyone sympathetically by the touching youth of

her small head, her fair fine hair, her
white neck, and drooping lashes.

But when encouraged she could speak,
and had a charm for every man. For the
young she had a youthful charm, all fire
and promise and delightful companion-
ship; for boys an astounding patience,
flattering them first by her sweet attention, and adding to this real words of
flattery and burning tangible incense till
they grew red and pale with worship.
But it was with men of age and experience that she had her greatest success—
men of means, men whose hair was grey
or white or falsely coloured, who had
outgrown all simple pleasures, including
also the happiness of family life, but who
could still find interest in youth and
novelty, or on the other hand in experience, but who were altogether ravished
when the two could be discovered together.

Of men of this description Serena had
an indefinite number ready to listen to
her and question her by the hour. They
discovered in her a singular treasure and

were prepared to hand her all round
their circle, years and philosophy having
cured them of the fault of jealousy.

Serena, having technically long lost
her innocence, and having since known
men of many professions, doctors, the
clergy, officers of the Army and Navy,
Americans, Frenchmen, and the equerry
of a Turkish prince, could through her
own extraordinary reticence—which
never drew her into the error of a recital
of her own life—combine the qualities of
youth and freshness with an engaging
philosophy and cynicism. She had
learnt, for instance, that many Italians
are indiscreet, that many Frenchmen are
to be trusted, that Americans lose their
way in an intrigue, and that Englishmen
are apt to confess to their wives. Her
discretion was the more extraordinary in
that, though she had suffered very truly
from time to time from numerous and
unpreventable desertions, she had never
at any time asked sympathy on these
scores from her dearest woman friend.
She was thus enabled to live cherished

and respected while drawing from life
all its experience.

With men whom she could trust, men
whose first fear was for their own reputa-
tions, she allowed herself to talk freely
and chastely of life; chastely, because on
no matter what subject her tongue wandered she had a singular instinct for the
perfect word that makes every meaning
palatable—freely because there was nothing she did not know. Had it not been
for her miraculous sense of secrecy, her
sphere of action would have been limited,
her talents would not have had full play,
for her family might well have cast her
out, and all who would then have come to
her would have come in the banal ex-
pectation of finding just what she could
give them.

But as hardly a breath of scandal
touched her name, not more than is in-
evitable and forgiven by all, accusation
of meetings and flirtations by jealous and
marriageable girls—and since no one had
ever heard of such discretion in a woman, she was believed to be what it en-

chanted everyone she should be—a delicious combination of wisdom and youth, of divining knowledge of men and total inexperience. Thus, isolated by her own reticence, Serena developed strangely. For, having no sense of morality, she did not condemn herself, and not condemning herself her conscience was stainless, her attitude towards herself and the world free of guilt, her affections sincere, her heart kind, and her freshness spontaneous.

Before she was yet eighteen her father died and poverty settled over the Blandishes.

"I will work," said Serena.

Her mother eyed her child with pleasure and compassion, and having regard to her talents, ankles, eyes, and wrists, suggested the stage.

"Does it not rather label me?" objected Serena.

"As what, my dear?"

"As what I should not be, mother."

Serena having preserved her reputation through worse tempests was not inclined to wreck it on a profession.

"There are academies," said her mother vaguely, "where the theatre is regarded as an art. . . ."

"But the trouble, my dear, is the money," she added. "The course might take a year, and God knows. . . ." The poor lady wept.

"Bread can be earned in one way or another. It does not alter the adventures of life," reflected Serena, and being of a tractable, affectionate nature she was reconciled without further objection to the profession her mother seemed to wish her to follow.

"As for the money," she thought without alarm, "with so many friends for whom I have done so much. . . ." She thought over the resources of her friends.

Her first visit was made upon a banker, a kindly man, in the prime of life, so rich that he had many calls upon his income. Every morning of his life he received a dozen letters asking him for money for some deserving charity, and

12

though he tore them all up and threw
away the pieces he felt the poorer in his
pocket for having received them.

"It is miserable," he said earnestly to
Serena, taking her hand sincerely in his,
"but for the moment you do not know
how I am pinched."

Serena excused him hastily and begged
him not to think of it again.

"But I must!" he insisted, "I shall
think of it constantly! I am tormented at
my inability to help you. If I could I
would load you with diamonds!"

"Oh, diamonds!" said Serena, realis-
ing that she had only asked him for a loan
of two pounds a week—and kissed him
affectionately and left him.

"My father," she began, on her next
visit, "is dead, and I am left penniless."
This lover, listening, paled.

He saw himself led into fabulous ex-
penditure. The house which he must
buy for her stood heavy in his mind, the
motor which he might long ago have
given her and never missed its price,
rolled before his imagination.

"The moment," he groaned, "is come when I must do what is right by her." But he stiffened. He would resist his upbringing and his training and his instincts and his pity, for he knew that an impulse, once resisted, never returns strengthened to the battle.

"Let but this moment pass," he thought, "and I shall no longer see her as young, pitiable, poor, and a victim—but as someone who probably has as much claim on another as on myself, and will not scruple to exact house, motor, and money from several quarters. No, no, it would be folly further to mix my affairs with hers. I might be in danger of forming a lasting responsibility. Here is danger. This is the signpost. This is one of the points in a man's career when he must show himself, worldly, ruthless, and decisive."

This while Serena, innocent and simple, pursued her tale, riches came near her and receded. And as she spoke the lover started; and as he listened his fears cleared from his mind. "Two

14

pounds a week," he heard her saying,
"for six months. That I may learn some
profession that shall make me independ-
ent."

For a moment his admiration of her
swayed his heart, for a moment he
wanted to cry to her, "No, no! That is
not how you shall be treated by me!
Listen to what I offer!" But the light-
ning thought struck him that what he had
not yet offered she had not yet missed,
and in the nick of time he answered,
"Two pounds a week is a good deal."

"I feel it is," replied Serena, with
sympathy and shame.

"I could manage two pounds for a
little while," he went on, "and we can see
how it works out."

Serena sprang to her feet and to his
neck, all her belief in life bright in her,
all her sense of the solidity of affection
deepened into conviction. The lover's
heart swelled with pleasure as he thought
to himself, "It is worth while to be kind."
And walking with her to the door of his

flat on both their faces their differing happiness was written.

"You must have a taxi," he pressed her.

"Oh no, I can walk."

"It is raining."

"It is so pleasant to walk in the rain."

"See, here it is!" he triumphed. "I rang and ordered it."

He closed the door of the taxi, and lingered bare-headed by the window.

"I am going away," he told her. "I am going abroad. Let me know when you have found your teacher and I will settle with her before I go."

"Ah," she sighed, looking at him sadly, not because she would miss his personality, but because the abstract thought of parting is painful to any woman. "Let me see you again before you go!"

He smiled at her tenderly and answered vaguely, signing to the driver to take her from him.

Once alone, at the end of the street, Serena opened her purse, and when she

16

had well shaken it seven pennies fell into her lap, her little comb, her mirror, and her lip salve. She stopped the taxi and got out.

"Driver," she said, standing below him in the rain, "if that gentleman who ordered you did not give me any money to pay for you it is not because he is ungenerous. He has just told me that I shall have fifty pounds in a very little while, but the truth is that at this moment I have only these seven pennies in my purse."

The taxi man looked at her stonily.

Serena tipped her purse upon the seat beside him. "You can have the seven pennies," she said, "the comb and the mirror. But even penniless and in your debt I must keep the lip salve."

"If the gentleman has such a kind heart," said the taxi man, "we could go back and get the proper fare."

Serena reflected. "It is easier to ask for fifty pounds," she said, "than for one and sixpence. And besides, I think he has just said good-bye to me for ever."

The driver looked down into her
lovely face, her anxious eyes. He put the
seven pennies into his pocket, but handed
her back the lip salve.

Alas, the next morning when she woke
up her mother brought her the paper
which contained the news of the death of
her generous lover. He had had a stroke
on leaving the theatre and had died within an hour.

"Is it not the gentleman," said her
mother, "whom you told me had be-
friended you and would help you to find
work?"

"It is," said Serena, "and indeed I am
sorry for him. But alas how hard money
is to get!"

"Money?" said her mother suspiciously, "you did not tell me it was a
question of money?"

"It is always a question of money,"
sighed Serena evasively. "I must find
seven and sixpence for a wreath."

CHAPTER II

POVERTY settled deeper over the Blandishes, and as it settled they learnt to keep
affection for the moment when it was
needed.

"You must work," they said again to
Serena, who sat in the window seat over-
looking the road, her head bowed under
this injunction. She was not bitter, but
reflecting.

"It is not," she thought, "that bread is
not easy to earn; but that it is not worth
earning for a woman of my youth and
beauty. In the pursuit of bread I shall
crumble my beauty, and when it is gone,
and I am eating the crust I lost it to
obtain, where is my kingdom? Where is
the glitter, the power, the fortune that
belong to my face?"

And while she reflected her mother
said again, "You must work."

"Let me think!" she answered, and her thoughts ran on—"I would have said, 'I must find a man and live upon his fortune,' but that I have seen the uncertainty of such bounty." Her eyes rested on the stone church opposite. "Where fidelity tires," she murmured, "where Nature gives out—the *legal* tie—Marriage!"

It was not a word she had looked at hitherto, but now in her adaptable way she faced it with courage and determination, and began immediately to fit herself for its benefits.

"Till now I have not used my heart," she said, reviewing her lovers, "and when I dare to use that in the security of marriage there is no reason to suppose that it will be inconstant. I am docile, beautiful, and young. And since what *seems* to be *is*—I am a virgin."

"Yet it cannot be very easy to marry," she pursued, "since with all my qualities no one has yet pressed marriage upon me. It may be that the system which I have pursued has been at fault."

20

At this moment a motor drew slowly past the gate, and a lady leaning out of the window to speak to her chauffeur, there leapt, as it were an emanation from her bosom, a little brown monkey in a yellow jacket.

Clutching at the door handle it slipped down the side of the car and was away up the garden path into the arms of Serena. The chauffeur followed, pursuing. The door of the car then opened and a lady stepped out.

The lady paused and stared at Serena as a great artist or a great merchant is allowed to stare upon beauty. On the roof of her car she had a caged peacock which she had just bought at the docks from an Eastern ship. At her home she had a gazelle, wild eyed with misery, and an Arab boy who had forgotten his language, but not one of these was as rare as Serena, whose face looked out over the brown head of the monkey in her arms.

"Is it possible," exclaimed the lady, overwhelmed by an instant desire to add

21

Serena to her collection, "is it possible that in such surroundings—Are you on the stage, my child?"

"You are astonished at the beauty of my face," said Serena, caressing the monkey, and looking at the lady in her turn with admiration. "But alas, it is set on no stage, and is in no limelight whatever. That reward which beauty should procure I am only too sadly aware I have not yet discovered."

"You are unmarried?" said the lady. "You are not engaged, you do not follow a trade?" For, unable to classify that which lay outside her own society, it struck her that she might make Serena her personal maid.

"I am not married," said Serena reflectively, her beautiful eyes resting on the lady. "But I do not see, do you, any reason why I should not be. As for a trade, I am loth to believe that beauty is meant to work. Yet it is true that I must soon come to some conclusion, for whether beauty should work or not there is very little money in the house."

22

The lady who thus admired Serena was a wayward, an eager, and an autocratic woman. She was not afraid of youth and beauty, for she had learnt to rest her weight upon the charms of experience. With eyes lined with life, with lips red as lacquer, a busy woman without judgment and with nothing to do, she hurried from enterprise to enterprise, searching industriously for original pleasures.

As she looked at Serena she discarded her first intention. This lovely, frail, and reflective girl would never make a practical maid.

"I will adopt you," she said eagerly. "But stay! First show me your ankles."

What a fool might have taken for insolence Serena recognized as majesty, and from where she stood inside the low window, obediently she placed each foot in turn upon the window sill.

At the sight of these slender bones and the arched foot in which they terminated, the lady was more than satisfied. "Will you come with me?" she said, and the jewels in her ears winked and glittered.

23

Serena cast a glance down the street in which she lived, and nothing in it appeared as radiant as the lady before her, and the shining nickel and scarlet of the car beyond the garden gate. At odds with her present, and believing in opportunity, she would have been foolish indeed to have refused such an offer. Whether the scarlet car might drive her to prosperity or misadventure, she would at least be obeying her instincts—to refuse nothing to anybody, and, while expecting little, to be prepared at any moment for the future that belonged to her good looks.

"I will come," said Serena gratefully, smiling with pleasure.

"I will take you for two months," qualified the lady, for being practical, her enthusiasm was often tempered with caution. "And before that time is ended you shall make the most brilliant marriage in my world."

"Is that easy?" marvelled Serena.

"Not easy, but with your face, possible," replied the lady. "Now if you will pack a little bag and say good-bye to

24

those friends whom I can see looking
from your windows, I will wait for you
in the car and we will start at once."

Serena, having kissed her mother affectionately, and having explained to her
the immediate solution of the future,
went down the garden path and stepped
into the car.

"The monkey has torn his coat," observed the lady, as they drove through
the streets. "I have been buying pets
for my household, and down at the docks
as the ships came in I found him in his
little jacket, and a parrot and a peacock
which are on the roof of the car."

"And she has found me also," thought
Serena, without resentment, for she was
glad to think she was starting on a new
life, even in company with a parrot, a
peacock, and a monkey. "As for the
monkey and the birds, both life and death
are assured to them, and while they are
not dead they ask no more than to be kept
alive. I, on the contrary, am conscious of
a hundred refinements of happiness, and

it is possible that all that I have missed hitherto will now be offered to me."

"What is it that you wish for most in life?" suddenly asked the lady, interrupting her thoughts.

"Happiness," replied Serena, with some hesitation.

"Is there no precision," cried the lady, "in that beautiful head? Happiness! Why not wish for death, for heaven, for fiddlesticks?"

"Money—to buy happiness," corrected Serena with docility.

"Money," echoed the lady firmly. "Security. That is to say, if you are a woman, marriage. And it must be a rich marriage," she pursued, eyeing Serena with suspicion, for she had heard that the middle classes often married for love and were permeated with sentimentality.

"Is it possible," thought Serena, listening attentively, "that all that I have ever lacked in calculation, firmness, and worldly knowledge will now be placed at my disposal? Am I to have a stage on which to shine, and an able chaperon

26

to direct my fortune, ignore my hesitations, and force the hands of my admirers?"

"Have you much knowledge of men?" said the lady.

"Very little," replied Serena cautiously. "I find them inexplicable and baffling."

"That is absurd," snapped the lady, who disliked incompetence. "You must get over that." And closing her eyes she lay back in her corner and went to sleep.

"No," whispered Serena to the monkey, which was staring at her with its unwinking eyes, "you and I cannot be companions. For the life of an animal is the most simple, and the life of a woman the most difficult in the world."

Presently they arrived at a house of brilliance such as Serena had never dreamed of. At the great street door they were met by three charming men.

"Here," thought Serena, encouraged by the sight, "here lies my future, here begin my opportunities." Smiling, she observed that the first was dark and worn,

the second young and blue eyed, the third
—when from her benefactress's manner
Serena realised that these were servants.

The monkey was put into a Chinese
jacket, the peacock into a courtyard, the
parrot into a cage, and Serena given a
little room of her own.

"In whose house am I?" she enquired
of the maid who brought her a can of
hot water.

"In the house of the Countess Flor di
Folio."

"Of what nationality is she?"

"I couldn't say," replied the maid.

The Countess Flor di Folio was a
Brazilian of forty-five, the cruelest age
in women, whether they be enemies or
benefactresses. She had the mind of a
child, the energy of a wild animal, and
the health of an immortal. She was no
snob, and though still beautiful and very
rich she had a delightful flair for bad
society. There had been a time when
the most exclusive persons had accepted
her invitations, but having everything in
the world that she wanted she had tired

28

of them, and her growing fondness for the
disreputable, the curious and shady, for
all quacks and purveyors of sham goods,
sham art, bogus literature, her passion for
imitation fur, imitation tortoise-shell,
imitated antiquity, had led her at last to
the pitch of appreciating an imitation
aristocracy, and with the cunning of a
child, which thinks it takes in all the
world, it had delighted her to palm off
bogus dukes upon genuine duchesses.
With the result that she now fed at her
table a willing menagerie of adventurers,
and a few old friends of standing who
could afford her reputation, could stand
the smell of counterfeit, and came because
they delighted in the artful pranks of
hungry bandits.

She adored the abnormal and the extravagant, snakes, Arabs, and hyenas.
Like a child she wanted to teach the
worm to swim in water, the fish to sit at
table, the dog to mate with the cat. Behind the house she had made a courtyard
garden, which now, turned to marble and
mustard weed, housed a wild gazelle,

thirsty and haggard at the haunches, the indignant parrot, the cries and beauties of the peacock, the monkey petted or deposed. Below in the kitchen lounged the sick Arab, wasting his days, he who had lately been the countess's Eastern playboy, filled the vacant chair at luncheon, and clamoured in delightful language for the food that went by in golden dishes.

Here came Serena, extravagant, unusual in her beauty, cherished by the countess, who now believed that she had a genius for adoption and could make something of human beings.

Here came Serena, guideless, undiscriminating, and with her for fortune her black past and her innocent mind.

"What can one do without marriage?" enquired the countess, when she had sent for Serena on the morning after her arrival; for this practical woman loved to strike at once.

"One can do nothing," replied Serena. "It is true that I have not yet tried very hard, but a very little experience has been

30

enough for me to come to that conclusion."

"It may be," said the countess, "that you are as intelligent as you are lovely. If that is so there is no reason why you should not have everything you want in the world. You are firmly determined to marry. There can of course be no two ideas on the subject. Some keep the desire secret, some openly deny it, some avow it; it is all the same. And though it is better to marry young, best to marry a rich man, next best to marry a distinguished man, it is better to marry a crossing sweeper than not to marry at all. There, in a few words, you have my wishes for you and my beliefs, which I am sure coincide with your own.

"In my house you will meet the most delightful, the most amusing, and fantastic men. Some even are batchelors. One of them may marry you. You must be careful, you must be clever, you must be cautious, and we will see what can be done for you."

"You are very good to me," murmured

Serena. And there was so little goodness looking back at her from the face of the countess that at her own words she grew bewildered.

"I have a final advice," said the countess warningly. "Not all marry who make love. In this house, as in others, there are men of all tastes and all intentions. Nothing is more pleasant when one is young than to dally with a man who is no use to you; and nothing is more wasteful. With you everything is a question of time. Your beauty, my discovery of it, your sudden appearance, your innocence and your freshness . . . these are intangible assets which must not be allowed to grow stale. Your brilliant engagement must follow hard upon your appearance at my table. Your career, unless meteoric, will not exist at all, for it is built upon no foundations. To-night I give a dinner party. I have already written several notes to whet the appetites of my guests and prepare them for a surprise. I will indicate to you which are the batchelors whose attention

32

and admiration you must engage, and by
the end of the evening I shall hope to
hear from you that more than one of them
have asked to meet you again."

While she spoke the countess appeared
to herself in a satisfactory light. She
admired energy, practical and immediate
action, and lucid explanation. In these
qualities she was at this moment excel-
ling. She saw herself as a business-like
theatrical agent arranging the contracts
of a Star, as a triumphant benefactress
whirling her protégée to success.

The effect on Serena was appalling.
She was far from being a triumphant
person, and those pliant and reflective
qualities which she possessed could ap-
peal to no inmate of this household. Her
desires had been for security and a sphere
in which she could pursue the docile and
adventurous pleasures of submission, and
where she need not work. That very
docility, equally affected by a pleading
lover or a sturdy benefactress, now led
her to accept success and a brilliant mar--
riage as her ambition: a difficult goal, a

33

prickly enterprise. But at the close of
the countess's speech, Serena's courage
was routed, her nerve shaken, and even
her beauty pinched and pale. The announcement of the evening party, the ex-
pectation of direct results, the sense of
hurry, fell like separate blows upon her
self-confidence. When the countess
pointed out the intangibility of her assets
she confirmed Serena's worst suspicions.
"Do not, ah, do not expect too much. I
am without weapons," she would like to
have cried. But she saw in the eye of the
countess an intolerance of weakness
which warned her to keep silent. Docile,
she determined to do what she could;
humble, she was anything but sanguine.

"You must have a dress," said the
countess to the fortunate and trembling
protégée—and, finishing her own toilet
with the disregard of a busy child preoccupied with an idea, they drove together through the streets in search of the
shops and the silks of Serena's dreams.

The countess, though not mean, was as
thrifty as she was practical. Her deter-

mination that Serena's looks should not be eclipsed by her frock was only equalled by her desire to be moderate in the outlay.

"Simplicity," she said unwontedly (for it was not her nature to be pompous), "is all that beauty needs," and stopping at a big store near by she bought her a little black frock such as Serena herself had occasionally been able to afford before her good fortune.

"That is delicious!" exclaimed the countess as Serena stood before the mirror in the fitting-room.

"It is true," thought Serena dispiritedly, "that I look well enough." And her sense of gratitude was so keenly developed that she forbore to think of the dear moment of extravagance, the flimsy and fantastic garment she had expected.

WONDER upon wonder rose before Serena.
Not that the plate which she ate from
should be gold, but that it should be gilt;
not at the brilliance of the countess's
clothes, but at the touching, the beguil-
ing imitations which she liked to pretend
would pass muster as fashion. To those
who are very rich, reflected Serena as
they shopped together, it seems heaven
to buy a little dress cheap. She did not
know how tired each section of society
grows of itself, how each longs, like a
coster girl on a Bank Holiday, to try on
the hat of the other.

"The very rich," realised Serena with
surprise as they ate buns together in a
tea shop, "do not always live very richly."
And again she did not know that there
are a thousand ways of being rich, and
that the only one which does not exact

36

thought, upkeep, trouble, and responsibility is having money in the pocket.

"If I were rich," thought Serena, "how well I now would know how to please those around me. What presents I would give, waterproofs to princesses, and vain and frivolous silks to poor girls who have no waterproofs." But she was wrong. For had she been rich she would have entered a complicated, charitable, and indebted forest from which the desires and needs of her late companions would appear a smoky and receding haze drifting ever more vaguely behind her.

"If the countess were to ask me," she thought, as they drove down Bond Street on their way home, "what I should like most out of these shops, I would say, 'Give me one object out of any window you light on, regardless of whether I need it. But let it be the best in the shop. For once let there be no compromise with price. Let me stretch out my hand and say "I will have that," and let no one reply "Certainly, but it can be copied in a cheaper material." ' The longing of the poor," thought Serena, "for nothing short of the best is sometimes overwhelming."

But the countess, as they drove on, asked her no such question, and Serena, who was occupied with reflections, passed between the shop fronts without envy and without resentment.

So the day passed and the evening drew on. Until at last, divided between anticipation and fear, astonished by her surroundings, uncertain about her dress, Serena descended the flight of stairs that led from her attic into the mirrored hall below.

At the foot of the stairs, in the hall itself, stood a man of charming appearance who watched her as she neared him. In his expression was fatigue, but in his manner, as he looked at her, was the grace and uncertainty of the great world she was about to enter. Returning his glance her heart grew calmer, for she said to herself—"After all, there are people of spirit and sympathy everywhere." She did not know how to greet this stranger,

38

and looking at him her face softened into a smile of friendship.

At her smile he grew graver, and when she stood at his side he said in an undertone, "I am Martin, the butler." To what she felt to be a rebuke she did not reply, but looking uncertainly from mirror to mirror that lined the hall around her, "These," she would like to have told him to reassure herself, as she saw the beautiful and familiar children multiplied upon every wall, "are Serena Blandish."

Pressing his hands against a heavy door leading from the hall Martin threw it open, and the hum of voices could be heard within. Serena approached the door, and trembled upon the threshold. As she hesitated she thought she heard his voice say low behind her, "You are right. There is much to be afraid of here."

The room which she entered was full of the gayest assembly. Fear, yes, lay in Serena's heart, but excitement and anticipation carried her forward. "Well I

39

knew," she thought to herself, "that there were doors which might open to me upon just such a stage as this; and how magical the impulse which caused the countess to adopt me."

"Come," said Flor, holding out her hand to the lovely creature. "This is the girl," she told those nearest her.

Serena, who had no pride, gazed back with pleasure.

"Whom are we waiting for?" asked Flor, counting her guests.

"Lord Ivor Cream," announced Martin behind her, and a tall young man entered the room with a quick step. "I am late," he said with assumed anxiety.

"A batchelor," said Flor to Serena in a low voice. "I cannot pùt you next to him. But remember that of all the young men you may ever meet he is the most marriageable."

Serena regarded him with curiosity.

"Does the countess," she thought with surprise, "imagine I can marry such a brilliant creature?"

40

'As the guests passed into dinner Serena drifted with the throng.

"Hush," she whispered to her beating heart, "many of these after all are men, and I have my beauty." And with beauty before her like a shield, she walked into the dining-room.

Martin touched her chair and his eye caught hers. In spite of his chilly air she thought, "I have a friend."

As she took her place at table, Serena realised that all those whom she had formerly known would have looked ill in this assembly; that even the banker, the Italian whom she regretted, would not have graced this table, and that she was breathing sharply in brighter air. She was in a new world, in which there was something which both chagrined and delighted.

Beside her, already seated at the table in a wheel chair, was a man of the very greatest age, in a state of perfect preservation, whose record was one of the legends of London. At twenty he had been the most handsome, at thirty the most promising, at forty the most licentious and distinguished, at seventy the most picturesque, and now that he had just celebrated his centenary, the oldest man in society.

"Here at least," thought Serena, with a sense of relief as at a respite from opportunity, "is no batchelor. Here no cunning, no caution is expected of me." Martin picked up a napkin she had not let fall. "I am to tell you from madame," he said in her ear, "that your neighbour is a widower."

"We are never at the end of surprises," said the Veteran, echoing her own feeling, as he settled himself in greater comfort, "I could not have believed that to-night I should have met so beautiful a young lady, nor you so old a man." "Perhaps not so great a distance separates us after all," murmured Serena politely.

"What! Yesterday I attained my hundredth birthday!"

"Though not twenty," replied Serena, "I am hard upon your heels. I am told that nothing is so easy as to grow old."

42

"It isn't so easy as you think," replied the Veteran, a little offended. "After sixty it goes much slower."

"Since sixty then you have lived more than twice my life," she said sweetly. "How much you must have to remember and to tell."

At this great opening he began at once, but he had not so much to tell her as she expected, for he had forgotten the years between twelve and ninety-nine. But he told her stories of his boyhood.

"And you have been married how often?" she asked.

"Three times, three times. Ah."

He smiled and shook his head, for he could not remember his three dead wives.

Serena looked about her as in a dream. The dining-room was domed. The walls of turquoise and gilt rose like cliffs. In the crushing heat, beneath the starry menace of the chandelier, a globe of living goldfish stood in the centre of the table. "Here is opportunity," she mused, "dazing, bewildering. From this table I may rise beloved of a cabinet minister,

a millionaire, a duke. Yes, an accident
may turn me from a waif into a duchess.
What a buccaneer am I," she reflected.
"What a soldier of fortune is every unmarried girl."

"It is always on the cards that a man
may be attracted," she thought, "even
kings. Even white hairs. It is on the
cards."

The guests, who were not nearly as
illustrious as she supposed, looked back
at her with admiration. The living goldfish, blinded with terrible light and
warming slowly in the water, dived and
stared at these creatures bigger than gods.
"Yet this world," she reflected, "is not so
simple, for I have not only to attract
them, but when attracted I have to hold
them off for another purpose." Such
double dealing was foreign to her nature.
She thought of the widower at her side,
who, free from the attendant who usually
accompanied him, was delightedly drink-
ing all that Martin could offer him.

"Is it possible that the countess thinks
him eligible? When almost in the same

44

breath she suggested that even Lord Ivor Cream might not lie beyond my possibilities. It is perhaps" (the thought struck her) "my neighbour's approaching death which makes him equal in eligibility with that brilliant young man." She did not know that the countess was a child, to whom all fresh ideas seemed alike of value so long as they were amusing.

Her glass was filled. It was Martin's hand on the napkined bottle, and Martin's voice in her ear. "The Countess's compliments," he said, "and you must talk to these gentlemen."

Startled, she looked up, and at the end of the long table the countess's black eye for a second menaced her. Turning in panic to her neighbour, she found the widower's cheek flushed, his eye full of tenderness. He had charm, she thought, with that blind charity of hers which had no sense of years or class. "I would have a refuge with him," Serena murmured, stabbed by the dart in the eye of the countess. "It would cost him nothing to marry me, and if I were in his position I would do it for kindness to another."

In her fright she was almost prepared to venture her weight upon this crazy bridge. Leaning towards him they talked, and she offered him her sparkle, her health, her hope, her vitality; fanning him till he thought he could bear again the dear winds of life. He grew eager once more. "I have had a long life, but it is not finished yet," he chuckled.

"It is never finished," she murmured with vague encouragement.

"Ah some day, some day," he replied. "But to-night I feel young."

His weak and aged smile touched her, and she reproached herself, saying, "I could as easily bear to snatch a baby from its cot as this old man from his coffin. Nevertheless I have implanted in his head the idea of a fourth marriage." And this was true. For not a week later his marriage was announced as completed without preliminaries to an American, dazzled by the chic of his great age.

46

On the other side of Serena sat one of those men who do not appear to have time for the conquest of a stranger, who seem to be going from one intriguing and wearying appointment to another, who glance at their watches frequently, who smile alluringly and yet with fatigue, who pique by their preoccupation, who are always leaving for the Continent, and whose secondary liaisons do not last longer than a fortnight.

As Serena turned to look at him she was aware of his tender and neglectful smile, she knew him as her brother in experience, her companion in outlook, her lover at a glance, her deserter at dawn.

Impelled by her familiarity with the type she was drawn by degrees into an indiscreet conversation.

"It is well for me," she said presently, "that though only nineteen I am fully armed against the dangers of your charm and your indifference."

"I hardly know," he began lazily, looking her in the eyes, for he made a point

of never listening to the spoken words of
women.

"You hardly know what I am saying,"
she finished smiling, "for you have no
need to exert yourself to listen. There is
always at the back of your affairs some
real or imaginary woman more important than she to whom you are talking,
and, though fading, you continue to exercise a provoking charm. You dissemin-
ate a sense of worldliness and an atmosphere of foreign cities which would
break down the morals, and even capture
the heart, of any girl as young but less
experienced than I."

As she spoke he started and looked at
his watch; and she too started, for she
realised her indiscretion.

"I leave at midnight for Venice," he
murmured.

"Thank heaven!" exclaimed Serena,
"for what have I been saying! And yet
if I had not spoken a word you would
have known me, as I know you, at a
glance. You the universal betrayer, I the
universal accomplice."

"I am leaving for Venice," he repeated abstractedly, for he remembered he had given no orders to his manservant. "But I shall be back in a fortnight and perhaps if you are still here——"

It would have soothed her in this strange company thus to hear again the familiar accents of a dishonourable proposal, had she not caught the strange and menacing expression on Martin's face. Reminded by this of her deeper designs, of the countess's warning, of the fine limit of her adoption, she smiled at him instead of replying, and rose with the ladies to leave the dining-room.

In the drawing-room, since no one at first spoke to her, she had time to examine those around her, and amongst them she noticed a lady of refined though distraught appearance, no longer very young, and wearing no wedding ring upon her finger. Meeting Serena's mild look the lady rose, and crossing the room sat down beside her.

"Yours is a new face in this house," she said solemnly.

49

"You speak," said Serena, "as though that were a misfortune for me."

"One is fortunate or not according to what one expects," said the lady, still more dejectedly.

"I expect to marry," said Serena, with a valiant smile.

"Then," said the lady bitterly, "you could not have come into a worse set of people, and with a vainer intention."

"Yet I left a society equally useless to me."

"The only class in which it is easy to marry is amongst the poor. With them a woman is a useful acquisition. With us she is an expensive, a superfluous adornment."

"You dishearten me," said Serena. "Though even as an adornment I would contrive to be as cheap as possible."

"It is true you are an adornment," said the lady. "You are very lovely, and if you could keep your confidence, and get engaged during the next week all would be well. But in this house, and in this atmosphere, you will not long believe in your powers.

"I myself have had a most unfortunate life. I have always been dignified and handsome, my eyes are fine and my hair is thick. At eighteen, at twenty, I was full of courage. From twenty to thirty I worked and hoped to get married; from thirty to forty I grew convinced that I should never succeed, and now at forty-five I find myself with really nothing to do."

"And yet," reflected Serena, "it is done every day. The lists of weddings in the papers, the pictures in the *Tatler,* the wedding presents in the shops, the brides' dresses at the dressmakers'——"

"It is done," said the lady savagely, "it can be done, but I do not know how it is done. There are wedding rings but I do not know how they are procured. In this life, believe me, there are no true batchelors. Look around this party, think of the men in the dining-room. They are either unhappily married, absorbed in a mistress, too poor, too young, or perverts.

51

Those who have mistresses are among the more eligible, but it has never been my luck to catch a man betwixt one mistress and another. You may have better fortune, but I assure you that it is only by the keenest enquiry and the most vigilant alacrity that one can contrive to meet a batchelor when he is temporarily free.

"As for me, I am extremely fatigued, and the word 'marriage' has come to mean an effort so wearisome that though I like to talk of it—indeed it is my only subject—I can no longer lift a finger or raise an eyelid to attract."

"But these women," continued Serena with gentle obstinacy, "who are here to-night, some of them are girls, some of them have but lately married, have you not known any of them, have you not discovered from them by what means they were married and what provoked the proposal from their husbands?"

The lady beside her shivered, and Serena noticed in her black eyes a look distraught and wild as though an animal were howling in her soul.

"You say there are no batchelors," remarked Serena, seeing that the poor lady was upsetting herself. "In which category then falls Lord Ivor Cream? He is clearly neither over young nor poor. Has he a mistress?"

"Ah, Lord Ivor Cream!" exclaimed the lady. "What a radiant spectacle! So brilliant, so eligible that it is painful to look at him. His smiles are farewells. He has humbled every daughter in Society. Excuse me!" she added, for a footman was handing her a note and she had paused to tear the envelope.

"Coincidences," she said as she read, "are not so rare as is supposed. Here is a note from a private information bureau to which I belong. Through some secretarial oversight they still send me advices though I allowed my subscription to lapse. After all, at forty-five I am not interested any more, but this may come in the nick of time for you."

She handed the sheet of paper to Serena who read:

"XY$_2$, after violent rupture, has

broken with RS; no one as yet installed to best of belief. Accuracy not guaranteed."

"XY2," translated the lady, "Lord Ivor Cream, has broken with Lady Rose Santacre, and has as yet no other mistress. Accuracy, however, not as you hear, guaranteed."

At this moment the door opened and the gentlemen returned from the dining-room. Foremost amongst them, and shining almost with his own brilliance, was Lord Ivor Cream who had no mistress.

"I will leave you," said the lady to Serena, staring at him with her haunting eyes. "I know there are times when it is better to have an empty chair by one's side. Besides, I do not feel well. Our conversation and your age have revived the past. I wish you well. I am sorry for you, for you are young and you have twenty years of disappointment before you. You should not have come here to find a husband. In houses such as these —I know them—night after night hope takes you in and disappointment drives you out. There *are* no batchelors. Believe, before it is too late. Men are not born batchelors any more, but these women with wedding rings, these modern vipers, give birth to married babies!"

She paused.

"But I am upsetting myself," she continued. "Forgive me. I am a spinster and a virgin, and forty-five. There are few combinations so perilous to the reason."

"You are a virgin?" said Serena.

"Certainly," said the lady with pride, and left her.

At that moment Serena caught the eye of Lord Ivor Cream. There was that in his eye which said to Serena, "Who are you?" and there was that in hers which answered, "I am what you see, young and beautiful." And those two messages passed, Serena closed her daring eyes and thought, "The opportunity is here."

"What," she said rousing herself, "do I fear this golden creature?" And fearing him, expecting him, longing for him, dreading him, she saw him rise in his chair.

Lord Ivor Cream rose in his chair. The eyes of the elder women were upon him, the hearts of the mothers beat with hope, but the young girls would not look at him. The chagrin he had caused them in the past was such they would not risk another hope upon him.

"Here comes fortune," said Serena, as he advanced the length of the room towards her, "here come position, triumph, and glittering security."

Flor's eyes were upon her, amused, delighted. Lord Ivor Cream took the vacant chair beside her.

Lord Ivor Cream had a manner at once wild and eager. Sometimes he started and drew back at some commonplace question, raising his head and staring as though he scented danger. Although not thirty he was supposed to be eccentric, and this added romance to his magnificent person. For he was an eligible of eligibles, and his nerves were ragged with suspicion. He was tall, and glossy, and

56

wild, and to catch him in marriage was as easy as catching a horse upon an open prairie. He could refuse, he could disappoint, he could lie without a pang. He could be resolute, courageous, skilful, or shifty. But his liberty, his liberty he was determined to defend.

"I have been looking at you all the evening," he said carelessly to Serena— and looked away from her.

Every eye in the room was upon them, and Serena, unaccustomed to use her gifts of attraction in such publicity, did not know what to do. She had her beauty, but that he had already seen. She had her curious mind, but what was passing in that she could not divulge. She reflected that what she did not say could not be misunderstood.

He glanced at her foot, which was perfect, at her hand which was divine: he reflected that she had the gift of silence —he liked the lovely girl, and rising, said low in his voice of a young monarch, without diffidence, without ardour:

"Will you lunch with me—in my rooms—one day?"

"And now," reflected the despairing bandit, "I have not yet spoken to him. What alchemy is there then in my glance which turns what should have been an honourable suggestion into one dishonourable? I am bent on marriage. I have by my side the most brilliant of young men. But it seems that I am fatally equipped for such an enterprise."

Should she lunch with him alone? She had taken his fancy for a second, and at a touch, at a misplaced word, he might move from her never to return.

"Will you come?" said the cold voice above her.

Where she might have shown indignation, where she could have afforded a refusal, her gentle compliance, her unconquerable docility were her enemies; she could not bear to offend, she could not endure to refuse, how then could she succeed?

"Some good may come of it," said the unguided child, and under his veiled

58

stare, and in the low tones of disappointment, she answered "Yes." Without
looking at her he named the day and the
hour, and she saw him walking from her.

"Is it possible," she said to herself,
"that he has already in his mind taken all
I have to give? It is, alas, not in my
power to refuse any man anything, but
how is it that they know so soon how
readily they may ask?"

As she watched the party break up and
gather round its hostess she found Martin
beside her with barley water upon a tray.

"You must leave your door open to-
night," he said, in a low voice.

She looked at him vaguely—and, preoccupied with the thought of her recent
defeat, watched the room empty of its
guests.

Flor came towards her, saying:

"It is too bad! I have just heard that
the peacock is dead."

"So soon?" said Serena wincing. As
the words left her lips she was thinking,
"What will become of me? This face
will fade, like the peacock's feathers, like

his bright tail and his wings in the grave. This wisp of spirit, as fine and bright as wire, will snap." She was tired, and the thought of Lord Ivor Cream discouraged her.

But the countess said to her with a smile:

"You have had your triumphs. What did Lord Ivor say to you?"

"He hoped," replied Serena truthfully, "that he would see me again."

When she went to bed she remembered Martin, and left her door ajar.

"For one should refuse no solicitation. No one in the world can have less than I, and I will leave every door ajar, not excluding that of my bedroom. In this way some good may come in—and little harm —for no one can deprive me of what I have not got."

So saying she got into bed, and as Martin did not come she fell asleep.

She awoke to find him standing beside her bed, a candle in his hand.

"I did not come to ruin you," he explained with his chilly air, and drawing up a chair he sat down.

"I am ruined already," murmured Serena, who was hardly awake.

"Ruin is a curious word," replied Martin, "and has no settled meaning. I must assume from your manner that you have had more than one lover. So long as you escape the perils of conscience it is only a partial misfortune not to be a virgin."

"Have you come to console me?" asked Serena, "to explain this life to me, to teach me how to succeed? Who are you, and have I a friend in this household?"

"I do not like intimate questions," replied Martin coldly. "And my friendship is almost more than you can ask for. To tell you the truth I have never found anyone worthy of it. As a butler I have learned to dictate and to observe, and as a human being, though I may take pupils I do not accept equals. As for the life that you are about to enter here, it is not simple."

"You are a strange butler," said Serena.

"Please do not handle my character," replied Martin sharply. "I do not allow it, and I cannot bear it. What I say, what advice I may give you, is suited to you and to your predicament. It appears from the countess's manner that you have come here to marry. Such an ambition amuses me, and I admit that I take an interest in your adventure. Have you enjoyed your evening?"

"The countess told me I had had my successes," replied Serena doubtfully.

"One must beware of such small successes," said Martin. "They make the time pass too quickly. One must not waste enthusiasm upon crumbs—but get the loaf."

"Alas," said Serena, "my difficulty is that in order to marry I must first attract, and once I have attracted I am never given time to remember that I must marry."

Martin looked at her reflectively with his black and melancholy eyes.

"Your position is not easy," he observed.

"Why?"

"It is not easy, when one has nothing, to attract good faith."

"Lord Ivor Cream," began Serena. But Martin burst into a sudden laugh.

"Mortals," said Martin, when he had finished laughing, "do not salt the tails of the gods. In that direction, my poor child, you will come by no good!"

"You don't believe then in his intentions?" asked Serena.

"For you he is good for nothing," repeated Martin.

"But he may tell me that he loves me," she argued.

"No one in the world loves you," replied the peculiar man.

"There is truth in that," said Serena. "It is a cruel world then?"

"One must not exaggerate," said Martin dryly.

"Then if Lord Ivor Cream will not love me, will he make love to me?"

"I don't wish to discuss that," said Martin. "I have my delicacies. But he will not marry you."

63

"He has asked me to lunch with him."

"I comment, but I seldom advise," replied Martin, and rose.

"You will suffer at my hands," he said, as he took up his candle, "and when you are lonely you can call that friendship." So saying he went out of the room and closed the door softly behind him.

CHAPTER IV

THE invitation which according to Martin, and in view of the gentleman's reputation, was nothing at all, was less than nothing at all. But Serena trod on air. Until she remembered the menace of Opportunity, which cries, "Take me! Embrace me! I am here to be seized or lost for ever!" And then she trembled and her heart beat.

The countess, who had such beautiful things, such a house, such jewels, such silks, knew the value of possessions. She knew what it was to receive gifts. She was kind, she was bountiful; she chanced to give Serena a silver hat. Another day came when she gave her a fur cape of ancient shape. Serena, who had no choice, wore both together, and she set forth to her luncheon, her lovely face looking out between summer and winter.

It was a fine day of thin blue air and gaiety. Chilly, to welcome the fur cape, bright, to give countenance to the silver hat. Yet Serena was trembling, pale, without courage, destitute. It is not thus that a lady goes to a new lover.

O glittering platform, marriage! To attain, turn, and bay defiance at the enemy! O fleeting time, years rushing, not to the grave, but to the unmarriageable age! That morning she had twisted her hair and made it tight and firm round her head with many pins. "For he will ask me to take my hat off at luncheon," she said, forewarned and pessimistic. Inexplicable young men, who admired her and would not be kind to her!

As she went down Piccadilly she was conscious of being followed, and this heartened her and gave her spirit. But when she lingered to satisfy her curiosity and the pursuer came abreast of her she was chagrined to find that it was an old lover of her own, who did not recognise her.

66

She looked into his face and he smiled without recognition, and the incident saddening her she turned into a chemist's shop for refuge.

"If I had caused him trouble he would have remembered me," she said to herself. "But as I took care to give him neither pain, anxiety, nor annoyance I have left no mark upon his mind."

In the chemist's shop were two customers. A baby leaned from the arms of his nurse and clutched at a bright bottle. The chemist reverently offered him a sponge instead, and the good baby accepted the exchange. Serena crooked her finger airily and the baby smiled. "That is a little earl," whispered the chemist, crossing himself. The earl stared at Serena and she at him. "A great godlike creature, with power to give and to withhold," mused the earl. Serena's thoughts were glittering and complicated. She put out a soft and insolent finger and stroked him on the cheek. "When you are twenty, earl, you will be cold and terrible, proud and desirable and out of

67

reach. When you are twenty I shall not care, because I shall be old."

The chemist had a musical box which he kept for such powerful babies. It had six little tunes and a lid which opened and shut. The earl took it in his careful hands and listened to the music. Then opening its lid he looked inside. The tinkle of music did not satisfy him. The shutting of the lid did not satisfy him. He turned it upside down. The bottom of the box could not appease him. He threw the box upon the floor and turned away. "We are always just upon the verge of pleasure," his eyes said mournfully to Serena.

"May I kiss him?" she asked timidly of the nurse.

"No," said the nurse, "we do not allow him to be kissed by strangers."

Reminded by this of her luncheon Serena turned to leave the shop, thinking of that other proud creature of whom also the world might justly say, "We do not allow him to be kissed by strangers." Kissed yes, but snatched and held never,

68

that goal of fierce, rich women, that glorious and envied man.

"Is there nothing with which I may
serve you?" asked the chemist.

"Unless you make a charge for the earl,
nothing," replied Serena.

At the door of the shop stood her pursuer, patient, with all the audacity of a
new adventure in his eyes.

He walked beside her. "Will you
lunch with me to-day?" he asked.

"You will ask me to eat epigrams of
lamb," said Serena warningly, "and
Maraschino soufflé."

The pursuer paused, and Serena
paused too and raised her eyes.

"You have made love to me before,"
she said. "I only stop you now, as one
stops an old friend who is about to tell a
story twice." The pursuer remembered
her. The colour rose in his cheeks.

"Walk a little way with me," said
Serena, who had no wish to press her advantage. And she started to walk fast for
she was almost late, yet soon she walked
slowly for her heart was beating.

"I have a dreadful task before me," she told her new companion. "I want to marry a man, who wants to make me his mistress."

"You want to marry?" asked the pursuer, delighted with her tact, and readier than she to forget his mistake.

"Such a girl as I has no other livelihood."

The pursuer bit his lip, for though he had never contributed one penny towards it he liked to imagine her as well furnished with a livelihood.

"Money," went on Serena reflectively, "is very hard to get. And affection is a strange thing and much more rare than is supposed. It is possible that it exists within the bonds of marriage. It certainly is not to be found without them."

"It is my experience," said the pursuer, "that the getting of money has little to do with affection."

"I can only argue," said Serena, "that a man who would be fond of me would not allow me to be without what I need," but even as the words left her mouth she

realised that they might be construed as a,
reproach, and to change the subject she
would have suggested that they should
meet again, had not that also struck her
as an invitation that her companion might
himself provide both affection and
money; therefore, colouring, she grew
silent. It did not strike her, however,
that her delicacy was her enemy.

"What is he like?" asked the pursuer,
"the man—whom you can have no
possible difficulty in marrying?"

"Fabulously rich, and experienced,"
sighed Serena. "Alas, what a difficult
combination." And struck by a sudden
thought she paused a moment and
glanced at her companion. "I cannot
suggest that I have done you a service,"
she said softly, "but if ever I have given
you a moment's pleasure I would ask you
to help me now. Is it not possible for a
man to explain to a woman by what
magic another man may be brought to
propose?"

"Love," replied the pursuer cynically,

71

who was beginning to think of his own lunch.

"Ah no," smiled Serena wistfully. "That is your joke. I see you will not tell me. Are you—I never knew—married yourself?"

"I am."

"And you do not remember by what behaviour on the part of your wife you were brought to offer her all your life and half your money?"

The pursuer paused, for he was near, too near, his club.

"When you put it like that," he said, "I must say that though I am quite well satisfied with my life, I cannot imagine, I cannot conceive, and I cannot remember why I did it."

"It is, then, magic," whispered the waif: and shaking her head, and smiling at him for his courtesy, she left him and hurried down the street. By this encounter she was not filled afresh with hope or courage. Bright with the cold air, and trembling with reluctance, she approached the door she sought.

"Does his lordship expect you, Miss?" enquired the cautious porter of the block of flats; for he was accustomed to bandits.

"I can't tell what he may expect," she replied, "or hope. Nor even what he may get. But take me up to him for I am cold." And as she stepped into the lift Serena reflected that had she been of his own society Lord Ivor Cream would have taken the trouble to warn the porter that he expected a lady to luncheon.

As she stood outside his door Serena tried to remember her beauty. But there was no looking-glass to encourage her, and the discrepancy between her glowing face and her humble heart was such that even her good looks grew less authoritative, less marketable.

"There is no marriage behind this door," whimpered her fears, and had it not been for the contempt and the suspicions of the porter she might have been ready to turn back, and enjoy a hungrier luncheon hour in a less brilliant place.

The door opened, however, before she could decide, and, wincing at the majesty of the manservant, she stepped into the hall. She felt his hands upon her cape, to take it from her.

"No," she rebuked him, "I cannot afford to lose even so much of my self-respect," and holding the fur tightly round she followed him into a room beyond.

Lord Ivor Cream did not even rise as she was shown in. He was signing cheques; the occupation seemed to Serena sinister. "One second," he cried, and turning round with his pen in his hand he smiled at her. "I have to give this note to the porter."

While she waited she saw that he wore a flannel collar that did not match his shirt, and feeling the circle of her silver hat pressing like a crown on her head she whispered softly to herself:

"It is true that he needs no feathers, but I all mine."

The meal was served. They lunched. The young man eyed this enigma, and restlessly he left the table from time to time and moved about the room. Easily,

74

by a few questions, he discovered her birth, her circumstances, her position with the countess.

She did not know what to conceal or what to confess. "Kiss me," he said when they had served the coffee. ("And now, heaven help me, I have to make my choice," thought Serena. "I have to deny him, that he may finally offer all.")

She refused.

"Kiss me," he said again with an assumed indifference, "or," he smiled to himself, "I will not ask you to lunch with me again."

Faint-hearted, the poor assailant watched him. She had no idea that his treatment of her was monstrous. How should she? She had no standards. She had never been asked in marriage, she had never experienced the behaviour of a man who does not wish to anticipate. Her keen and piteous sense of justice demanded that she should pay for whatever was given her, and her humility valued her kisses at the price of a meal.

"I offer you," the countess had said,

75

"more than a dozen young men who are able to bestow marriage. Go and extract it from one of them, preferably the most brilliant."

Serena wished for no better end, but as she had indeed expected, she saw no way to an immediate triumph.

She might deny him. He would not ask again. What she might withhold he would not sufficiently care to pursue. He was world-worn, he was aged in his youth, he had invited her out of an idle whim, but in his eyes there was little audacity, no enterprise, no conquest. He had no wish for virile authority. He was half indifferently preoccupied with his own eternal escape.

If she persisted in her refusal it seemed to her certain that she would never see him again. Then how could she marry him? Yet if she kissed him she had been told that he would not marry her.

"There must be some rule of thumb!" she exclaimed, her beautiful eyes roving round the room. Virtue could not guide her. Virtue might in its ignorance have

76

known how to act. Her heart did not guide her, for none of these rich and insolent young men had troubled to set it beating. And while she vacillated, arguing where she had no arguments, planning where she had no plans, she was lost. He kissed her, and they sat down upon the sofa.

There, sitting beside him on the sofa, her heart hammered and her cheeks were burning. She had lost, but her incurable expectancy of immediate adventure was upon her.

"Alas," reflected Serena, when later in the afternoon she sat at tea beside him, "that one can only be at ease with a man upon the pillow. All that goes before that is hedging and fencing and mystification. Only when there is nothing left to desire and nothing more to conceal does he cease to misinterpret me. Alas, alas," sighed Serena, who had lost, "that one can only speak the truth to a man upon the pillow."

Lord Ivor Cream was restless. He

moved behind her with long strides, put his cup upon the mantelpiece, his plate upon the piano.

He had taken what she had not offered, and what he had barely demanded. He did not know why she had lunched with him nor what expected, but from long habit his mind turned to his cheque book, and from prudence he fingered the Treasury notes in his pocket instead.

"Diamonds?" he said to himself, as he watched her innocent face, so at peace with him and herself. But diamonds too he rejected, partly because on a child who seemed to possess nothing diamonds would gleam as an imprudence, and partly because he had no intention of giving them.

He paused as he walked, and standing beside her he said with curiosity:

"What would you like most in the world?"

"To marry you," she replied sincerely.

With a look of horror he sprang from her, and silence reigned in the room. So imperious was his habitual manner, so cold his eye, so abrupt his silence and lightning-quick his decisions, so equipped was he with all the weapons of defence and the means of escape, that such a wish had hardly ever been hinted to him, even by the most desperate, the most courageous of mothers.

"Did you come here with this intention?" he ejaculated in rough and jagged tones.

"Only with the hope," corrected Serena mildly. "It is expected that I should marry, because of my beauty, and because I have no other future. That is why I accept the invitations of batchelors. That I may say to myself that I have left no stone unturned."

There was again a silence.

"Marriage," whispered Lord Ivor Cream, shuddering visibly as he spoke, "is a word which I do not use." And so overcome was he by this utterance that he sank into a chair. Serena, seeing his pallor, hastened to pour him out a fresh cup of tea. "Drink this," she said, "you are unstrung. But of me you need

79

hardly be afraid. I have no confidence in myself, and, though I may hope, I expect nothing of anybody. And seeing how it distresses you we will not speak of this again."

"No," said Lord Ivor, staying her with his trembling hand, "now that the word has been spoken——" He groaned slightly and slipped a cushion under his head. "There is something bizarre about danger. For once let me speak of it. As you say, I could not well begin upon a less threatening personality. I grow too closed within myself. I have long felt the necessity of a confidante."

At his sudden air of weak though friendly confidence Serena, if flattered, grew depressed. "Alas," she said, "it is not when a man is thus at his ease that he proposes."

"Think, think," said Lord Ivor, "what a fearful position is mine.

"Besieged!" he groaned, and buried his head in his hands. As an admitted besieger she did not misunderstand what he meant.

80

"Since my youth, since my boyhood, I have had to endure this. I was too rich at Eton, too rich at Oxford. To the lure of my riches was added that of my title, my lands, my houses, my position. No one has ever approached me sincerely, no one has ever taken me by the hand without thinking of my pocket. I have never dared to live like other young men, to be free and open, to make friends where I chose. I suspect the whole world. I suspect my relations. I suspect all young women, all young women—ah—"

"Drink your tea," said Serena.

"—all mothers," he grew even paler, but recovering a little he went on, "all men in want of position, my tradesmen, my servants, my villagers. I try to hide my name. I go about under assumed names."

"It cannot be so bad as that," said Serena pityingly. He lifted his ruffled head and his eye was as wild as a wild bird's.

"You suspect me of mania?"

"No, no."

"Of a monomania then. It's true I'm afraid of that too. How can I be sane when I have never lived as you have lived, never been regarded as every human being has a right to be regarded, with indifference, that blessed indifference that gives privacy."

"But has there never been any woman who truly cared for you?"

"My mother is dead," said the young man bitterly, and he rose and stared into the mirror above the mantelpiece.

"It seems to me," said Serena soothingly, "without in the least pressing my own position, without for a moment suggesting myself as a remedy, that from the hour that you marry you will cease to be desirable as a husband. You will be relieved at once from all the mothers and all the young women in the world. Your servants, your tradesmen, and your villagers will deceive your wife instead of you, and you will have earned for life the undying gratitude of a lady whom you have enriched."

For a moment her adorable simplicity

82

attracted and touched him, but he was in love too with his own newly expressed and gorgeous sorrows.

"The lady whom I enrich," he said mournfully, "would never be grateful. That is the last emotion likely to bloom in her heart. With riches such as mine are reputed to be she would never consider anything sufficient, neither her allowance, nor my presents, nor the state which we might keep. I am past marrying. I am a fable. Women cannot see me for my glitter. I am like a man walking in a fire of wealth, so that his features are hidden."

"Although he expresses it very well," thought Serena, "he is a little unreasonable. For how willingly and how easily I might spare him much of his discomfort."

She rose to go. And he took leave of her, forgetting, in his sense of her having asked too much, that there was anything he might owe her. And she took leave of him, forgetting in the enrichment of a moment of sympathy, the intention with

83

which she had come. She was possessed
instead, as she walked under the lighted
lamps in Piccadilly, by the vision of both
combatants in the battle—on the one side
the army of Flor di Folio, and her allies
—on the other the Pursued, the rich and
lonely victim.

Full of pity for him she arrived at the
countess's house. To Martin who opened
the door for her she exclaimed im-
pulsively, "I have made a new friend!"
For she believed in the dim magic of the
evening, that she had a triumph to relate.

"Are you engaged to be married?"
said Martin coldly.

She was silent.

"A lady who stays to tea where she has
been asked to luncheon," said Martin, "is
never engaged to be married. But I hope
at least that if you have not a ring upon
your left hand you have one upon your
right?"

Serena admitted that her hands and
her pockets and her future were alike
empty.

"When I give advice," said Martin,

"I like it to be taken." And he pointed out at length how complete had been her defeat.

She struggled with speech.

"Tears!" he exclaimed with derision, and he drew an electric swinging bulb towards her eyes that he might search for that which glistened.

"Do you think it better to be a woman than a man, Martin?"

"Oh *no,*" said Martin, "I am not such a fool!"

"What a curious afternoon," said Lord Ivor Cream, now recovered. And he related it briefly to a companion.

CHAPTER V

In the night, influenced by Martin's words, Serena dreamed of diamonds. And when she awoke she determined to go and look for herself what kind of woman it was who obtained these badges of value.

"That is the image in man's mind," she thought, when she had reached a shop window behind whose bars gleamed diamonds of all waters, "of his own generosity. These are the standards of his opulence. But are they in reality to be bought and sold? Is it possible to receive them as a present? I will stand here a little and see what men and women go in at the door, what charm that I know nothing of, what beauty greater than mine, can procure for itself the diamond out of the promise."

And while she was standing in the

street looking in at the window she caught the dark eye of a Jewish salesman who watched her from between the cases.

"Come in," he said pleasantly, joining her upon the step of his shop. "I see you take an interest in jewellery. There is nothing that I wish to press you to buy, but if you would care to sit here for a few minutes I can show you some beautiful pieces."

Serena, who accepted every invitation, went into the shop and sat down beside the counter.

"That I may not enter upon false pretences," she replied, "I must tell you that I have not a single penny in my pocket."

"I do not look," he said, "for pennies from you. I think that, charming and attractive as you are, it is from another pocket than yours that I might be paid."

"Alas," said Serena, "you judge by the fineness of my hair and the colour of my eyes that I am worth even one of the finest pieces in your centre case. But you are wrong. For though a great deal has been said to me about diamonds I cannot at present find money to buy myself a new pair of shoes."

"People of my religion," said the Jew, "instinctively know the value of everything. I am therefore well aware of the selling power of beauty. How is it that you, who have a beauty rarer than I have ever seen before should be standing outside the greatest jeweller's in London without a ring on your finger? That you have not a penny in your pocket does not surprise me, for the most bejewelled women are often penniless. Women, unlike men, seldom have money upon their persons."

"But they have it in the bank," sighed Serena.

"No," replied the jeweller reflectively. "Women, like savages, often carry their fortunes upon their wrists and fingers. Often I have suspected that a charming creature with a fortune about her neck dare not allow herself the luxury of a full meal. It is better after all to eat a bun and a sandwich than to have to pawn a necklace for meat.

"But come," he said more briskly, "let

us see why it is that you have not the
jewels you deserve. There is some slip.
There is some link missing."

"The link that is missing," said Serena,
"is that I have not the first jewel."

"You are right," said the Jew ener-
getically. "You are right. It is my own
theory. It is my own theory exactly.
Never have I seen a man purchase diamonds for a woman who was not already
covered with them."

"Diamonds!" said Serena, looking at
the show cases wearily, "Let us talk no
more of them. To what fabulous women do men give diamonds?"

"To those who already have them,"
replied the Jew. "For if you had a little
money you would get more, if you had
but one ring men would add to it others;
but to have nothing, to be penniless, is not
to excite sympathy but disdain."

"What then can I do?"

"As you may have noticed," he replied,
"I am something more than a salesman
with enthusiasm. I am also a theorist, and
prepared to act on my theories. Never

before have I seen in this shop a girl so beautiful and so conspicuously empty-handed. I will provide your first step to fortune." He walked to the show cases. "I will adorn you with your first jewel, and we will see whether these lovely creatures breed, and whether one diamond can beget another."

Serena rose and followed him to the cases.

"No," he said leaving the window and going to a drawer, "these are better. These are as valuable, but more modest. We must not frighten the first donor with a sense of competition. Here is a ring which will give you a stamp of value combined with an air of honesty. You may wear it for a month and we will see what comes of it. I take my chance. If you are not as honest and unfortunate as you appear to be I lose my ring and gain no client. Yet I think I see from your face that it is your very honesty which is too often at fault. You appear to me to be tractable, docile, willing to please, unwilling to offend. Believe me that is not the way to work if you are to bring me in profit on my ring and yourself a comfortable array of jewels upon your person. My experience of twenty years of diamonds tells me that it is not to ladies of your expression and temper that I am indirectly enabled to make the largest sales. A look of pride and a jealous mouth, ill temper, suspicion, exigence, are the qualities that bring me custom. Believe me, men buy more diamonds to placate than to please."

Thus advising her he slipped the ring upon her right hand, and after admiring it a moment he took up a pen that he might enter her address in his book.

"You think," said Serena bewildered by her good fortune, "this will also help me to marriage?"

"Marriage!" exclaimed the Jewish salesman, throwing down his pen, his face changing. "You said not a word to me of marriage! This indeed alters the complexion of my loan. I did not look forward to your finding one husband but twenty. I did not suppose that your pur-

chase would end with an engagement
ring and a band of platinum, but would
begin with rose diamonds and end with
cabochon emeralds. Marriage! O foolish girl, look what may be yours! Jade
boxes with jewelled hinges, lapis cigar-
ette holders, pearls, strings, ropes of
pearls. Marriage! Whom can you
marry? The rich will only marry the
rich, or the well born or the well known.
Were you even on the stage you might
succeed. But poor, humble, and without
notoriety, what can you do, who will
marry you?"

Serena, who was looking at the ring
on her finger, did not reply.

"You may try it," said the salesman,
less agreeably, "for a fortnight. I have
less faith in you now."

So saying he took her address and
bowed her from the shop.

Serena, fingering her ring, wandered
down the street. She had not taken much
notice of his tirade, but she pondered his
remarks upon her too tractable disposition.

"I see that I have faults," she thought, "but perhaps I shall soon meet with someone worthy of my nature. Surely it must be more endearing to be charming than expensive."

Yet she was beginning to suspect that this was not the case.

At the end of the street Serena met a young man whose father had just left him fifty thousand pounds. It so happened that the young man had expected seventy thousand pounds, and therefore he was feeling that the addition of fifty thousand to his own previous capital of four hundred left him rather poorer than richer. He was a very old friend of Serena's, and they walked together through many streets, overjoyed at seeing each other.

In his pleasure at meeting so old a friend the young man commenced to praise her. He talked of her beauty, her loyalty, her discretion, of all she had taught him of women, of the gentle hand that so young a creature had had in his education. At such praise Serena's spirits

93

rose. Her difficulties seemed no more than a jest. Without showing him the ring she told him laughingly of the advice given her by the Jewish salesman.

"I am, it is evident, not extortionate enough," she smiled. "You, for instance, have never made me a present in your life. I believe it has never occurred to you."

"I never have," he avowed frankly. "You make me ashamed of myself. What you say will be a lesson to me. I will certainly never be so mean again in my relations with anyone else."

"So even as a teacher I am unsalaried!" thought Serena, and so odd did the private heart of man appear to her, that she laughed gaily and bade her friend good-bye in high spirits.

Finding that she had after all a penny in her pocket Serena climbed to the roof of a passing omnibus and sat down in a far corner.

"Men and women treat each other in a very peculiar manner," she thought. "The world is full of intimacy without

94

friendship, love without service, admiration without a single wish that the object of it should be happy. My friends, for whom I have done a little, would do less for me than the veriest stranger. In fact I can hardly believe that they would do as much."

At this moment a man sat down upon the seat beside her.

"My beauty, which should be a constant capital to me I seem unable to invest. Indeed I have nothing in this world but a little black dress, this silver hat, and this fur cape which the countess has given me. If I wear a diamond upon my finger it is because a stranger has loaned it to me." She pulled off her worn glove to look again at the ring. "Yes, it is in strangers that I must place my hopes. From strangers I may expect any generosity. As for one's friends one cannot ask them for anything. They consider they have given everything in giving friendship."

All this time she had been perfectly aware that the man on the seat beside her was not looking at her. As this situation was a little unusual she turned towards him to see what he was doing, and saw that he was reading a novel called *Friendship*.

She could not see his face, which was turned from her, but pointing to the title of the book she said: "My experience on this subject is very wide."

The stranger turned up his coat against the spring wind, but either he had not heard or he wished to continue his book without interruption. He made no reply, and Serena sank again into silence and reflection as the bus passed from street to street.

"I have no more money," she thought to herself as she looked at her bus ticket, "and I must have long outrun my fare." At this she would have left a seat on which she had no special reason to remain but that she was lulled into an instant's fantasy that it was her husband who sat beside her.

"Oh, that I might reply to the ticket collector, 'My husband will pay for

96

me,' " and glancing at the unrevealed
man pressed so familiarly against her she
felt for a moment all the stability that she
imagined lay in marriage.

"What a strange thing it is," she
thought, "that I cannot procure this
simple pleasure, nor find this natural
security." The voice of the ticket collector broke in on her thoughts. She
showed her spent ticket without moving.

"My husband will pay for me," she
said aloud serenely.

The stranger closed his book and put
his hand in his pocket. Serena felt that
he was looking at her; then without a
word he passed up a penny to pay for her
fare.

"Why did you say that?" he asked in
rich, deep tones, when the collector had
left them.

"Because I wished that you were my
husband, and then I fancied that what I
wished was true; and so, losing fear, I
tried the words aloud. Do not misunderstand me. I am not as yet attracted by
you. I have not seen your face. But I

97

am without a husband, and of all things in the world I should like to be married."

"And will nobody marry you?" he asked.

"Nobody," she replied, "has ever made the slightest suggestion of marriage to me, and from what I can observe there are a great many charming women in the same unhappy condition."

While she was speaking, the mind of the stranger beside her had leapt into instant activity. She could observe his inward commotion in the stiffening of his attitude.

"I have always longed," he muttered, "to meet a woman of courage!"

And with an air of spiritual affinity rather than of intimacy he laid his hand upon her knee. When he turned his face towards her she could hardly endure the ardour of his gaze. His eyes, nose, mouth, moustache, and chin bristled with temperament and character.

"Are you Irish?" she said involuntarily.

He waved his arm.

98

"Not Irish!" he said, as one who would not be pinned down, yet would not deny. "Not Welsh. Not Scandinavian, or Latin, wholly. Not from the North or from the South. Many lands contributed to my birth," he said.

While Serena was trying to decide whether it was his father who had deceived his mother, or his mother his father, and how in any case this would enrich his birth, he went on:

"You are beautiful, but that is nothing. I am dispassionate about the beauty of women. I look at it with my eyes but I keep my heart in my breast. But courage —I can only look at that with my heart! Where I see courage I know there is Passion," (he made the word ring)— "and a rare soul. You are filled with that fire of life, beautiful young lady."

"Who are you?" said Serena softly, carried away a little by his praise.

"I am a Lover!" he replied, in tones like a hidden furnace.

"Are you married?" asked Serena

who remembered she had her interests to protect.

"Yes—no. I am neither married nor free!" he exclaimed impatiently.

"You have a mistress?"

"I have many mistresses," he replied, staring fiercely and warmly into the past.

> "O daughters of dreams and of stories,
> That life is not wearied of yet,
> Faustine, Fragoletta, Dolores,
> Félise and Yolande and Juliette,——"

"But are you now free of them?" breathed Serena as he paused.

"Being dead, child, they can never free me. Age cannot wither these immortal women. But my heart is free, though my imagination is wedded," he said hastily, seeing her downcast look. "And my hand," he added, feeling that she liked precision. "You all but proposed marriage to me, wonderful child!" he cried enthusiastically. "I will marry you!"

"Can you support me?" enquired Ser-

ena, emboldened by the occasion to be
her own guardian.

He drew his heavy brows over his
deep eyes and smiled a grim and fas-
cinating smile.

"You too," he said, "have known the
necessity to eat. For you also meat and
bread have not flowered naturally upon
the wayside. Ah, this makes you perfect.
This completes you! Your boldness was
not that of foolish innocence and ignorance, but you have known life, poverty,
and hunger, and uncowed you demand
that you shall not know them again. I
have another test of your perfections. I
see you wear diamonds. Are you a
maiden?"

"No," replied Serena.

The stranger was silent a moment.
And then in tones which trembled with
emotion, he said "A miracle!"

"A miracle," he repeated. "A woman
who, to such a question, replies 'No,' in
such a manner, without preface or
apology. Without bravado. Who
taught you such candour and such sim-

plicity? Who left you untaught, that you might preserve such beauties? Who bore you, who bred you? Out of what circumstances do you come?"

"I was born near the docks," replied Serena, "and I have been adopted by the Countess Flor di Folio."

"What a history in that sentence," he commented softly. "You were born near the docks—where from the East the ships come in, and amidst tar and foreign words and spices, the Lascars sit with folded arms and spit into the eternal Thames."

"Are you an author?" asked Serena, enchanted with his translation of her previous surroundings.

"I am a Poet," he replied. "You were born near the docks, and you have been adopted into Mayfair. A trembling, ruinous, lovely greenhouse, a company of orchids waiting for the Gardener. The name of your benefactress is the strangest flower of all. Where does she live?"

"In Berkeley Square."

He smiled divinely at her.

"In Berkeley Square! Does her roof leak?"

"I hardly think so," said Serena.

"Her roof leaks. Believe me! *All* their roofs leak. *All* their roads lead to ruin. *All* their pockets are empty."

"That is strange," said Serena. "For she had all the appearance of riches."

"The appearance of riches is the last thing that deserts the bankrupt. Once a woman has been rich it lingers like scent when the bottle is empty. You do not know how poor your new world is. The pearls may be still unsold, the footmen still cluster about the unpainted street door, the food may still be delicious, the hats still arrive from the unpaid milliner. These women cannot draw in their horns. The debts are too vast. They rightly disdain economy."

"But if the luxury is there," objected Serena, "somebody pays."

"No, nobody pays. It is not paid for. There is a vast marginal moment between riches and ruin."

"Then who are you that you know so much?"

"I am a Money-lender!" he replied with exultation.

"Is trade good?" asked Serena with interested sympathy.

"Trade is abominable," he replied. "But beautiful. I lend but I do not receive. I am dirt-poor, yet I give to the rich. And what I receive in return are their miserable diamonds."

"There are then women who will sell their diamonds for a meal?"

"There are Russians who will sell an emerald for a bus ride. Women who sell their principles for an invitation. Duchesses who sell houses on commission. Convicts who sell their papers at the prison gates."

"But——"

"You are right. That has nothing to do with the case. But sell, sell, they must. Jingling diamonds for coin in their pockets. They pay in precious stones, in beads, like savages."

"Diamonds will soon cease to have their value?" asked Serena, anxiously.

"Beauty will never lose its value," he replied in a different tone, and looked at her white and gloveless hand. "You set loose my ideas," he said with tenderness. "You encourage my words. I forget that here beside me I have the loveliest jewel—of candour, honesty, and beauty. Let me see your ring. I will give you a better than that. Who should know the value of diamonds if not I! You have not told me your name."

Serena gave him her ring and her name, (with the prayer that she too might receive a ring and a name).

"It is a modest ring," he said. "You had it from a lover?"

"I never had a lover," said Serena sadly, "who gave me anything. I had it from a stranger an hour ago."

"Alas, poor child, you specialize in strangers," he said, still examining the stones. "I told you I was a money-lender, a poet, and a lover. I am all that and more."

105

"What else are you?" murmured Serena.

"I would not be a thief," he replied, "if I could have utilized my other gifts," and so saying he vanished down the steps of the omnibus with her ring.

Hurrying to the head of the steps, she gazed down the street, but it was empty, the money-lender vanished, and Serena, having lost husband and ring, got off the bus and prepared to find her way home. Having no money she had to walk many miles before she could see again the comfortless and charming features of her friend Martin.

Climbing the marble steps at length she sank wearily into the footman's chair in the hall.

"Martin," she said, "I have been lent a diamond ring and been robbed of it. I am unfortunate, and tired."

"If you continue in this way you may in time," said Martin, with a cold smile, "get on the countess's nerves."

"More likely," said Serena, searching his face, "that I should get on yours."

"That is certain," said Martin, smiling more than ever. But seeing that she was really tired he patted her on the shoulder.

"Am I not kind to you?" he demanded.

As the days went by Serena grew uneasy
under the eye of the countess. There was
impatience in that eye, and a desire for
results. At luncheons, at dinners, Serena
redoubled her efforts, and the young men
who swarmed about her made every sort
of suggestion but never any which she
could report with a certainty of giving
satisfaction. It was with difficulty indeed
that Serena could withstand the continual
importunity, and there were times when
she knotted her brows over the perils of
assignation.

There were days when the eye of the
countess seemed to sharpen, and moments
when Serena came as near being suspected
as she had been in her life.

"Where is the flaw in her?" wondered
the countess when she had a thought or
a moment to spare. And from time to

time she looked searchingly in Serena's face. But truth and innocence reigned there, for the conscience of Serena was unstainable, her thoughts free from duplicity.

It could not be denied that the countess's enthusiasm was cooling. Martin, who was the first to observe it, said warningly, "You must make hay, my child, while the sun shines."

"I am doing all that I can," said Serena distractedly. "But though there is ardour in plenty to be found, marriage seems as far off as ever. And why should the countess, who loved me, grow tired of me?"

"Where you are loved for no reason," said Martin, "you are dropped for no reason."

At the end of the fortnight the ring was due to the Jew. Serena, who should have gone before, returned to the shop to confess her loss. The Jew in a fury demanded eighty pounds, or he would apply to the Countess Flor di Folio. Serena

going to Martin for advice found him in
his worst mood.

"I don't give advice," said Martin, for
he saw that there was none to be given.

"I don't ask you for money," said Serena, frightened into a small insurrection.
For once Martin was stung.

"Money I would have given you," he
said more simply, "but I haven't any."

"Then what shall I do?"

"Take a long view," replied Martin.

"How will that help me?"

"Look at the stars," said Martin,
smiling at the ceiling, "and remember
that we all die."

He returned to the gold plate which
he was cleaning, and held up a polished
spoon that he might the better search for
his grey hairs. None knew whether he
was afraid of age or welcomed it.

His worn and charming face stared
back at him from the spoon. He fingered
a hair on his temple. He reflected. Nobody on earth knows what were the reflections of Martin. It may be that he
did not really care for women. It may

be that he had real pity in his heart, or it may be that he liked to have his finger in every pie. One cannot know his mind for he would never admit anything, and had no intimates. "I have not learnt," he had once grimly replied to an offer of friendship, "how to enrich my life with others."

To be a butler, to be a king in the kitchen and a king's minister in the dining-room, to quell a subterranean tumult, and direct the whimsies of an upstairs world by tightening the manner, to know how to put a guest at his ease or out of it by a glance; like a king to allow oneself a rare freedom of speech, and like a king to know how to deny it to others. "I believe you are God!" Serena had once cried with desperate rebellion. "I too sometimes feel like 'that," replied Martin.

In short, to be a butler one needs mystery. Whatever words Martin allowed himself his thoughts were hermits.

Serena, forced back upon her own wits,

once more reviewed the resources of her lovers.

"It is not a moment," she said, "when delicacy of mind can be weighed against a downfall. The Jew has allowed me a week, and at the end of the week he will tell the countess. The countess will turn me out and I shall go back to failure, poverty, and lack of opportunity just at a moment when I am beginning to appreciate the charming possibilities of riches.

"It is true," she further thought, "that before the countess's adoption I had very little success in my applications for a small sum of money. Yet stay—was it not the very smallness of the sum which hindered me? To ask for a few pennies, a pound or so a week, is contemptible and likely to meet with failure. According to the new doctrines now around me the more one possesses the more one is likely to receive, and it may also be true that the more one asks for the more one will meet with success. I now need eighty pounds. I will ask for a hundred, a request that will command respect and also give me a margin of twenty pounds."

And at that moment she remembered Sir Verilees Poncham.

"Ring me up," he had once cried in his love, "and ask for a hundred pounds before tea, and another hundred before dinner." And at that time Serena, transported with pleasure in such a nature, had flung her arms about his neck and thanked him unendingly.

Sir Verilees Poncham was not quite of the society in which she now found herself. He was an excellent and ageing physician who had the fortune to attach himself to the outskirts of Royalty, and when first he had offered himself as her lover Serena had laughed as she caught sight of his white hair and long beard, but she had not laughed aloud for fear of hurting his feelings. "What," she had said to herself, "is there no incorruptible age?" And almost as she began to laugh she had reflected that white hair never seems white to the wearer.

She remembered now how his love for

113

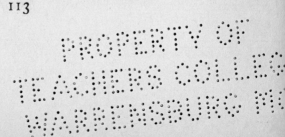

her had made him generous. Sometimes he would buy her cigarettes, sometimes he would promise her a pearl necklace, sometimes send her one of his free tickets for the opera, sometimes tell her he must buy her a horse.

Serena, remembering such kindness, went to see Sir Verilees again, her silver hat, her helmet of conquest, upon her head, her fur cape wrapped around her shoulders. He was delighted to see her and to hear her accounts of her good fortune, he was amused at her story of the Jew and the loan of the ring, but when she told him that she had lost it, and of her predicament, it seemed to her that all at once he had recollected some perplexity of his own, for he began there and then to wear a cold and preoccupied air, and she could not at the moment find courage to make her request. "But I will write it in a letter to him," she decided.

On reaching the countess's house she slipped quietly upstairs without confiding in Martin, and sitting in her bedroom she wrote the letter.

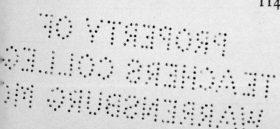

"My Dear One," she wrote, "You have so often offered me so many gifts, you have so often generously begged me to accept so much money which I have refused, that I am daring to ask you for a gift of a hundred pounds for a special purpose. I told you of my misfortune with a diamond ring. The Jew who lent it to me threatens that he will expose me to the countess at the end of the week. From what Martin says of her she will be intolerant of my folly. I beg you to help me."

She posted the letter. She awaited the reply.

Day after day went by and she began to wonder whether Sir Verilees was ill or had been called away to some case in the country.

But Sir Verilees, at the other side of London, after many angry moments, had discovered his note of indignation.

"After all I have given her!" he succeeded in saying.

"Yes, after all I have done for her!" he exclaimed, for he found this a better wording: it did not specify so exactly that his goodness to Serena had lain in gifts. He found on looking into the matter that Serena had no hold whatever over his affections. His indignation with her therefore increased from hour to hour.

"What, ask me for money, like a common girl! Like a girl from whom one could expect no delicacy! What a sad and horrible disillusionment."

Serena, conscious of having meekly asked little where much had been freely offered, waited patiently and anxiously for the post. The week which the Jew had allowed her was slipping by. "Though," thought she, "there is no shadow of doubt but that he will give it to me. How could he have the heart to refuse? How safe I am with him. How much he has promised me. And then too I have some hold on his care and consideration."

When the letter from Sir Verilees arrived at last it contained his magnificent refusal. Serena, crushed, held it breath-

less in her hand while she felt the torrent
of her humiliation burst over her.

"Everything depends upon the point
of view," she murmured at last.

"I thought it natural to ask. He thinks
it natural to refuse. It is not perhaps a
question of who is right. It is possible in
all things for everyone to be right." But
though unembittered by this experience
she was bound to weep.

"Diamonds," she sobbed, "he too spoke
of diamonds. I cannot understand what
he meant by his generous offers. Is it
possible that they were in the nature of
exclamations of admiration? How often
have I thanked him unwittingly, seeming
on the very verge of a charming gift, and
have I ever actually received it? No,
poor as I am and without luxuries, and
rich as he is and growing richer from
patient to patient, he will not allow that
he has one duty towards me except in the
promise of his fabulous diamonds. Is it
possible," she wept, "that diamonds are
but a metaphor? The motives of man
are mysterious, and his speech to me is a

strange language. I thought I knew him,
I thought I pleased him, I thought he
loved me, but it is evident that I did not
understand his private heart."

She looked at the letter again, believing that her recollection of the sentences
must be false. "Your request is odious,"
she read. "You ask me to forfeit my
illusions."

Sir Verilees, in writing the letter, had
omitted all the steps of gradual indignation, aided by the secrets of miserliness,
by which he had arrived at the final
virtue which had dictated the letter.
While Serena had remained in the simple
and trusting attitude in which she had
made her request, he had travelled
through countries of the mind where he
had gathered fortitude to refuse her,
reason and justice to sustain him in his
refusal, and even (by a hypothetical statement of the case of a friend) wifely
counsel to lash him to further indignation.

"My answer must emphatically be no,"
he ended, "though I am prepared for
118

your anger and conscious of your mis-
understanding. I am a physician, I hope
of some repute, and I owe something to
my own ideals, to that banner of my belief
in womanhood which I am prepared to
carry unstained through life."

"It is extraordinary what one can come
to love," reflected Serena, who with her
naturally buoyant temperament was fast
recovering.

"On first meeting him I thought him a
preposterous old man. But I rebuked
myself, and reflected that there is good
in every man, and that his white hairs
ought not to render his love ridiculous. I
succeeded in feeling affection for him.
Now I find him little better than my first
opinion. The truth is," she finally reflected, "that a woman will love anything,
from a pekinese dog, a drunkard, a wife
beater, to such a man as he who writes
me this letter. I do not wish to flatter
myself, but my true experience is that
my own heart is the kindest I have yet met
in the world."

It was not long before she succeeded

in detaching herself completely from the letter, the episode, and from her sense of humiliation.

"It is not my pride," she said, "which dictates that I shall never see him again, but my condemnation. I cannot allow my pride to be the sufferer, since I consider it less painful to have asked for money than to have refused it."

With this thought she went downstairs to tea with the countess.

"SERENA," said the Countess Flor as Serena entered, "I am just going out, but I want an account of your debits and credits.

"What are your successes?" asked the countess.

At this her unstable, her unreasonable valiance deserted Serena. She was at once aware of other standards. Looking into the coal-black eyes before her she saw that she had no grounds for good spirits.

"It is a success," she said, to cover her emptiness, "to be young and beautiful."

"Blondes don't last," said the countess, straightening a black eyebrow with her finger. "They fade. Have you had a proposal?"

"Not of marriage," said Serena reflecting.

"Of what then?"

"There are always," said Serena cautiously, "suggestions of love."

"We are surrounded by them," admitted the countess. "Who has said he loved you?"

"Alas, few people," said Serena, quoting Martin, "feel love."

"Nonsense," said the countess sharply. "With your looks you should be able to report better than that. Your beauty has made a flutter but the flutter is subsiding. I sent for you to-night to tell you that you must act. If there are suggestions of love about you must utilize them. If you don't make use of your novelty while it exists, then soon you will be stale."

"Ah," murmured poor Serena, struck by so practical a statement, "then what will become of me?"

"God knows what becomes of the girls who don't marry," said the countess. "They don't stay in my world. Now listen to me. When you first came to me I thought your beauty alone would get you a husband. That was a mistake, for you haven't done enough with it. Your conversation too is limited, and you do not seem to realise that your responsibility as a guest is as great as mine as a hostess. Those who do not contribute to a party detract from it, and I have noticed more than once that you create a certain silence about you. Are you shy?"

"No," said Serena, trembling, "but so many of my private thoughts and ambitions are difficult to express."

"How absurd," said the countess, "to think of using your private thoughts in public conversation. You must suppress them, and after a little practice and experience you will find that they no longer trouble you. What kind of powder do you use?"

"None," said Serena.

The countess looked at her more closely. "Astonishing," she remarked. "But it is not right. Though you look very well, it is against nature not to use it. I will get you a box of my own. Come, courage! You are really lovely, and I am not unreasonable. With my

123

experience of blondes I know that you have a beauty which cannot endure, and I am all the more eager for your immediate success. It will delight me if you triumph. Think what your life might have been, and what it is and may be. I will give you another chance, and a better setting. To-morrow I will buy you a new dress. Be gay. Gaiety attracts. Be gay, but serious in your intentions. Make haste, take the name and fortune from one of my young men, and then you will see what life is. I give you a month from to-day, and then I must hear of your engagement."

"The Jew gives me a week," thought Serena, "and the countess a month. What shall I do with the rest of my life? For she does not know," mourned Serena, "that no one will ever marry me. Not one, not one of her young men." And listening to Flor, and listening to her own thoughts, she lost courage and grew bewildered. Flor's counsel was terrible. Flor's aims unrealisable. "I haven't the secret," she murmured half to herself.

"What?"

She raised her head like a little doe at bay. "Tell me," she asked the countess, "how it is done? I must admit to you that I do not know, and that when a man looks at me with admiration in his eyes I am at a loss how to reply. If a corresponding warmth creeps into mine he goes too far. If I remain cold he loses interest. If I—" she paused discreetly, "allow him to kiss me he asks me to lunch with him alone. I cannot believe that this is the highway to marriage."

"It is *not*," said the countess with warmth. "I should have thought it would be obvious to you that you must keep your kisses till after you are married."

"On what grounds then can one refuse?"

"On what grounds? You astonish me. What reasons need you give? Have you no instinct then of self-protection?"

Serena, who knew that she had none, remained silent.

"You had a mother," said the countess,

125

"you had surroundings, you must have had friends. Are you not aware of the ordinary rules governing a girl's conduct? That nothing must be given away, not one finger tip. That lips must express every provocation but must not kiss. That eyes must look every assent during the coldest of denials——"

Serena leant forward eagerly to catch the treasure as it dropped into her ears.

"I must go," said the countess. "I am late as it is. I stayed only to have this little talk with you, that you may know what I expect of you, what I am prepared to offer you, and the limits of my patience."

After this terrible statement the benefactress was gone, and the benefacted remained alone to ponder her benefactions.

"I must marry, marry, marry," tolled the frightened heart. "For after this month I see nothing, nothing, nothing." And Martin coming in found his protégée in tears upon the sofa.

At sight of him Serena dried her eyes, for she remembered that the only tears a

126

man approves of are those caused by himself.

"Martin," said she as she recovered,
"our mistress is a terrible woman."

"She is a child," replied Martin.

"Even children break their dolls," said
Serena. "How are the animals in the
courtyard?"

"Some dead, some dying," said Martin. "But the Arab is alive."

"Humans are tough," replied Serena.

"Misfortune has given you spirit," replied Martin.

Serena fell into despair.

She learned that distress could wake
her before the dawn.

"I am helpless," she said into the foggy
darkness, when not a cold beam lay upon
the walls. "I have but one life, and in
that I have no success," and her newly
woken spirit, damp and weak like a chick
in the egg, was unable to fight for
courage.

Then, the day breaking and growing,
she would go for sympathy to Martin.

But Martin liked to simplify his horizons. "The only real grief is the loss of those we love," he said. "And poverty too is disgusting." But he was busy, for there were preparations on hand for the reception of a princess.

"What is she like?" asked Serena to distract her thoughts.

"She is green with age," said Martin, hurrying about his work.

"It is curious," reflected Serena. "Men seem to be angry with women for growing old."

All the guest rooms were being opened. It was possible that the princess might bring friends. It was well known that she sometimes arrived upon a visit surrounded by a little court for which she begged house-room. The countess looked on with gaiety. She had given the invitation, and now she waited to see what would come of it. If it was to be a house-party, it would be ready-made for the hostess, and they would all be strangers to her. For the princess's friends

128

were never to be found in any recognisable society.

"You will see an odd collection!" she said to Serena.

The princess, who came from Paris, arrived in the station omnibus, having omitted to look for the cars that had been sent to meet her. She had very little luggage, no maid, and eleven friends.

"What a mercy this is the biggest house in London," said the countess as she kissed her.

The princess, who was not nearly as old as Serena had expected, wore a white travelling hat and long white veil, a leopard skin cloak, and white shoes with gold heels, in which she had crossed the Channel. Her friends, who were all men, wore between them seven Persian lamb collars. Expecting great cold in England they did not take off their coats. Flor was delighted. She laughed when she looked at her dozen guests. She adored a certain kind of eccentricity.

Martin was grave. He knew that he would have to find articles of clothing to

supplant those mislaid by the eleven gentlemen in packing. Also it was his task
to discover from among the trunks and
suitcases of the eleven, which shirt and
which waistcoat the separate originality
of each had intended for to-night's dinner. After he had served the cocktails he
went upstairs, and was in no mood to be
waylaid by Serena.

"Come to the pantry at midnight," he
said. "And then I shall be in a position
to tell you which of these gentlemen is a
bachelor."

The princess also was a little grave.
She had left her unpublished manu-
scripts in the train, and the early evening
was spent in telephoning, and the dinner
much delayed.

In the upper part of the house all was
turmoil, and Serena crept about in a delightful flutter.

"Have you a pair of scissors?" asked a
dark young man who leant half dressed
from his doorway. Serena found him a
pair.

"Come in," he said, holding his door

130

open. "It seems a waste of time to take this shirt off, and if I did I have no other. The cuffs are frayed. Can you trim them for me with the scissors?"

When she had done so the young man kissed her. "I am told that in England all women are platonic," he said. "I am your brother."

"I am glad," said Serena. "For you are certainly the youngest and the best-looking of the princess's friends."

"I am already a little drunk," he said, "and that is why you find me charming. When I am sober I am shy, and as my doctor forbids me to drink with my meals or soon after, I have to do the necessary stimulation beforehand. Living with the princess is very hard work, and travelling with her even harder. As I am neither a poet nor an artist I am considered to be practical, and thus I have become the courier of the party. To tell you the truth we have lost one of our members, and the most illustrious. I notice the princess has not confessed as much to the countess, but we expected to arrive here

fourteen in number to-night, for Count
Montague D'Costa (who has been mislaid) had with him his secretary."

"What is Count Montague like?"

"A most mysterious and silent person.
When he speaks it is in a mixture of bad
Portuguese and the vilest English. The
princess would be prepared to adore him,
but it may be the barrier of his language
that causes him to be distant with her.
She has never encountered such opposi-
tion before. At first it drove her into despair, and then into the extremes of love,
but now she is so exhausted by his continual gravity that it is possible she is
even a little relieved and rested by his
momentary loss."

"It may be," thought Serena, "that
every woman has her Martin."

"At any rate," said the young man as
he finished fastening his collar, "she is in
good spirits. Were she not she would
have called me to her room before this.
For she asserts that I am the only member of this party who does not think of
his own poems or his own paintings every

132

time she provides an illustration of misery. Excuse me. I am about to tie my tie. It is a moment of great importance to me, and one at which I like to be alone."

Serena left him and went back to her room to look once more in her glass. She had little vanity, but what little she had was awake to-night, for the countess had bought her a new dress. It was not easy to see her reflection in the mirror, for Flor had covered it with red birds and branches squeezed from a tube of paint, and varnish in imitation of lacquer, and the little creature in apple-green taffeta peered at her like a nymph caught in a scarlet jungle, her silks and ribbons held back by beak and thorn.

Serena's lips were scarlet, her face was powdered, her dress divine. She was a member of the countess's world; she had been kissed by a charming young man; for once she was full of confidence. Suddenly she thought again of the kiss and paled. It might be that he who had kissed was the only batchelor of the party, and in that case—"How soon one forgets," she thought, "rules which are not true to one's nature, or obvious to one's common sense."

When the princess came down to dinner she wore heels of such extravagant height that she had to balance entirely on the ball of her big toe. High up above her long neck her eyes blazed and her red hair raged. She was dressed in white velveteen with a wreath of monkey fur around her hips.

"What slaves we are to fashion," she said, sitting down and kicking off her shoe. "If there had not been a lift I should have had to walk down in my stockings."

Other guests invited for her entertainment began to assemble.

"I cannot stand," she said to them. "My feet hurt me," and when she went in to dinner she left her shoes behind her on the floor. Martin brought her a footstool.

Flor, in high spirits, looked round her party.

Besides the princess and her eleven friends there were a dozen other brilliant creatures of known eccentricity. An Armenian who was not sure whether his father was his mother's husband or the Turk who made her a widow, two or three young men with charm, two or three young men with money, a duke's son who brought the Argentine heiress to whom he was engaged, and his sister, who brought the billiard professional to whom she was engaged, a parasite or two from low down among the legations, and a celebrated dressmaker who brought with him the loveliest of his mannequins. When Serena caught the eye of this girl she knew she had a rival. A rival in beauty, a rival in desolation, a creature lovely, well-displayed, but unsuccessful, with an enamelled expression, a haughty manner, and a soul in panic. Her dress was more beautiful and scantier than Serena's, her hands were slim with an accidental breeding, on her finger was an audacious sapphire, the size of a cherry and made of glass. Round her neck was

a heavy rope of pearls, and she gazed at
the princess's white velveteen dress with
amazement.

"Manila," said the countess, nodding
to her across the table, "you are more
amusing than ever." She was referring
perhaps to Manila's garment, for the
white face that bowed stiffly in reply
grew even sterner with embarrassment,
and the red mouth that just moved in
deprecation was neither witty nor
amused. Manila glanced at her master
to see if her response had been in good
form, but seeing that he was not looking at her, she took up her fork and ate
her food with care and grace.

"You have no idea," said the princess
to the table in general, "what a strange
creature you have missed. Count Montague D'Costa, who should have joined
us at Calais, is the one defeat of my
career. He has a heart of steel and a
resolution of granite, but I am not so re-
vengeful as to say that he has a temperament of ice. He is romantically rich and
almost a hermit. He has estates in the

136

Argentine, oil in America, Portuguese royal blood in his veins, and a house in Paris. All this I learn from his secretary, for he is unable to complete an entire sentence in English, French, Russian, or Italian, which are the only four languages that I really understand."

"I hope we shall see him," said the countess.

"Cuckoo," said the princess to the young man whose tie caused him such grave moments, "have you telephoned to the station master at Dover to know if anything has been heard of Count Montague?"

The young man rose, leaving his untasted soup, and spent the next four courses of his meal in the telephone compartment.

"I cannot afford a secretary," said the princess, "nor a maid. But Cuckoo is very adaptable. I have taught him the art of packing, and how to telephone with patience and self-command. But we were talking of Montague. I must tell you," she said turning to the duke's

137

son, "that he is the only man whom I have never conquered. And now I despair of ever conquering him, for what you cannot do with a man on the first day cannot be done at the end of a dozen months. Women, it is true, can be worn down by attack, but if a man is not taken by assault he does not recognize your existence."

"I can hardly believe——" began the duke's son laboriously, with a distant compliment in view.

"Oh, at first I was rebellious!" went on the princess, brushing him aside. "But now I am content to install him in my affections as an ideal for ever. And then it has given me a taste for silence. I can sit in his company for hours, and think beautiful thoughts, and he will never once open his mouth to disturb me. Such a gift is rare," she said, looking round the room. "I can see that none of you have it.

"You have a butler," went on the princess in French to the countess, "whose face I remember when I was here

138

before. He is not unlike Montague. He
has gravity and charm. What a delight
it must be to have one's life managed by
a specialist!"

"He is excellent in many ways," said
Flor in her burning accent of Brazil, the
r's like little sparks, the l's like molten oil,
"but of course, like all these people, he
requires managing." Martin, who had
been brought up in Paris, handed her the
salad. It was a peculiarity of Flor's that,
except from the shape and colour of their
appearance, she did not know one person
from another. She had no idea that
Martin was a mystery, but she could ac-
curately have described his hair as dark
and his height as six foot; she knew
Serena was lovely, but not that she was
candid; she knew, for she had been told,
that the princess was an Original, and besides she could feel the buffets of her
originality as it struggled and kicked between her own organising hands. And
her energy leant out towards these buffets
and struggles and she liked them, though

they were not her own mode of self-expression.

Flor did not care for intimacy or books or the revelation of character, but she adored energy, success, and red-hot action. Thus Martin, filling unseen the enormous gaps in her character, was able, like a directing motor, to run the machinery around it.

Cuckoo, exhausted by the telephone and famished, dropped into his seat by Serena's side.

"Is he found?" asked the princess.

"No word of him," said Cuckoo, munching the toast from a little rack while he waited to be served.

Martin, who handed him a dish, whispered to Serena, "The Jew is in the hall and wishes to see the countess."

"What shall I do?" asked Serena, growing pale.

"Ask him to marry you," said Martin coldly, for the evening had got on his nerves.

Serena's eyes filled with tears.

"You are hungry," she said to the

young man beside her, "but I am in distress." Cuckoo, his mouth full, saw the tear in her eye. Putting down his fork he pressed her hand.

"You kissed me," she faltered, throwing herself on his mercy, "and though I know very well that a kiss is never the expression of kindness, and not always of desire, yet you seem so friendly, so helpful, and so practical——"

Cuckoo glanced at his plate of food with apprehension. "What is the matter?" he asked simply.

"I borrowed," she replied. "And what I borrowed I lost. The creditor is in the hall."

"But I have no money," he objected, "the princess pays everything."

"I do not want to pay, but to postpone," she replied. And told him the details of her difficulty.

Cuckoo rose. "The telephone——" he said vaguely to the princess, and left the room. Serena waited for him with a beating heart, and a glance of apprehension at the countess.

"I have arranged matters," said the young man, returning in a few minutes. "He is an excellent fellow. He will not press you again for a day or two. I have no prejudice against Jews, and his manners were not at all bad."

"What did you say to him?"

"I had to tell him that I had just become engaged to you and would soon be asking him to supply the ring. 'What, another ring?' he said smiling, and had the good taste not to congratulate me. 'Yes,' I said, 'another. And I suppose you are going to make me pay for the first?' 'I am afraid I must,' he said seriously, 'or we could compromise over the price?' 'Oh, we'll not quarrel over it,' I said with the beam of a poor fool who has just tied himself up for life. 'But at any rate you don't get a penny out of me till you see the engagement in the *Times*. I won't pay a debt, buy an engagement ring, and lose a wife as well.'"

"And so?"

"So, as I haven't the money to buy a ring I haven't the money to get married.

142

And he won't see the engagement in the *Times,* and that won't strike him as odd for another ten days."

"Then you *are* a batchelor," said Serena, half to herself.

"It's the cheapest thing to be. And even that's not very cheap."

"Nothing is cheap," said Serena suddenly, "except unmarried young women."

"Oh come now!" said Cuckoo. "Are you angry with me for having said I was engaged to you?"

"No, no," she said, her eyes smiling on him, "but I cannot help thinking how much I should like to have a permanent defender."

"Any one would defend you," said Cuckoo admiringly. "You have only to set the right way about it."

"Ah," said Serena eagerly, "and what is that?"

"I don't know," said Cuckoo, "I can only recognize it when I see it."

At this moment there was a slight stir, and the duke's daughter fainted.

Martin and the billiard professional carried her from the room, and Serena, at a sign from the countess, followed her.

"It was the heat," said the duke's daughter vaguely as she lay upon a sofa by a window that opened into the street. "Don't make gaps in Flor's party," she said to her fiancé and at her request he and Martin returned to the dining-room.

"I am very much annoyed with myself," said the duke's daughter faintly to Serena. "Bert doesn't like scenes," and her thin face flushed slightly with chagrin.

"He cannot but be sorry," said Serena soothingly, "that you are ill."

"Bert hates emotion," replied the invalid, "for it disturbs his accuracy."

"But he is not playing billiards now."

"He is always playing in his head. You know he is a genius. Did he appear critical of me?"

"Oh no indeed! Couldn't you tell by his manner?"

"His manner is very deceptive. I myself am constantly deceived by it. I have

only known him a week, and am but engaged since Friday. I very much doubt
——" And she burst into tears.

"Oh what is the matter?" cried Serena,
kneeling beside the sofa.

"I am afraid he won't marry me,"
sobbed the duke's daughter.

"That," said Serena, "seems incredible.
You, with your birth, your setting, your
diamond ornaments, your air of having
castles in the background, your net-work
of relations, your cousinship with Royalty——"

"What a mistake you make," said the
other wiping her eyes, "to suppose all
that makes me eligible. Do you know,"
she continued, prepared to burst into
fresh tears, "that I am twenty-nine, that I
have lived since I was seventeen between
London and the Riviera, and that this is
the first time I have ever been engaged?
Even now it is so recent that he has had
no time to buy me a ring. Should he
throw me over before I have known the
weight of an engagement ring on my left
hand I shall never be able to bear the dis-

appointment. I am so emotional. I cannot help it! Each time I cry out of sheer
gratitude and relief I observe his eye turn
to glass, I hear his voice wear an edge,
and I know that any day I may try him
too far."

"If he hates tears you must not cry."

"We are as we are made: and tears are
my special outlet. Alas, I imagined that
once engaged there was an end to war-
fare with all the world, an end to intrigue and deception, and the keeping up
of appearances."

"Not till the wedding day," said
Serena thoughtfully. "And even then
there should be settlements."

"Of what are you talking?"

"Of security," replied Serena. "And
you?"

"I am talking of nothing in the world
but the enviable, oh the enviable status of
marriage!"

"Often," said Serena, "I have difficulty
in understanding the plainest of prob-
lems. So much, so very much, is not
what it seems. But that you, the brilliant

146

daughter of a duke, cannot achieve the status of marriage, is beyond me."

"You spoke of my cousinship with Royalty, my network of relations, and my setting. Do you suppose there are many batchelors who are willing to take on the burden of that? To keep me is more pompous than keeping a stable of race-horses, and not half so much fun. Duke's daughters are at a discount. They cannot marry upwards, there is nothing to marry. If they marry downwards, as I am trying to do, their surroundings appal and bewilder the commoner without giving pleasure. Even a visit to my father entails expense. And when after marriage my father proposes to visit his married daughter (as he would very often, for our castles are not central-heated), then think of the drain on the resources of the son-in-law."

"Does your brother find it as difficult to get married?" asked Serena.

"Oh no, for my brother gets the only benefit of our family; he will one day be duke. And that still goes for something.

But I, oh I have had the most wearisome difficulties, the bitterest mortifications, the most fatiguing intrigue."

At this moment the door opened and Manila entered.

"I have been sent," she said, with her bleakest expression, "to find out how you are."

"Come and sit with us," said the duke's daughter, and Manila swayed across the floor to the sofa in her professional manner.

"Have they finished dinner?" asked Serena.

"They are having coffee," said Manila.

"And so," thought Serena, "my position is not unique, and even this brilliant creature has the same fantastic difficulty in mating. What a revelation! For I could not have supposed that her engagement was other than a scandal. Instead of which it appears that it is her greatest triumph."

"Tell us," said the duke's daughter to Manila, "tell us—as we are on the subject—you are not married, are you?"

"I am single," replied Manila primly.

"Tell us, then, what are your difficulties, and why you do not marry?"

"I am interested in my profession," said Manila, "and I have not yet decided to give it up."

"Bosh!" said the duke's daughter. "I have been too long in this battle to believe that."

"I could marry to-morrow," said Manila, tossing her dark head, "if I chose to give up my art."

"If we don't believe it," said Serena gently, "it is only because we are so sadly experienced. But tell us about this wonderful opportunity. Have you really found someone who loves you so much?"

"There is a gentleman who comes to the showroom," said Manila, at bay.

"But has he proposed?"

"I have not allowed him to commit himself. But he brings me chocolates, and he looks at me in a way——"

"I know that way," interrupted the duke's daughter. "It will lead you to the river at Richmond, to a box at the theatre, and then it will lead you to bed."

"I am an honest girl!" said Manila, outraged.

"I am honest too," said the duke's daughter. "I was brought up to be. But it is all the same when you want a husband. I suppose virginity is so much taken for granted that it is not even an attraction. One might as well dispense with it since it cannot be advertised. I am twenty-nine, and it is an outrage that I have never had a lover or a husband."

"Ah, but now——" said Serena.

"I am engaged!" cried the duke's daughter, her face lighting. "It is so recent that I had almost forgotten it. But ah, Bert, Bert, if I can only get you to the marriage day!" She rose and walked restlessly to the window.

Serena went up to the willowy Manila and put her hand on her arm.

"I am sure you are right," she said softly, "to have such confidence. It is perhaps lack of confidence which makes my own campaign so unsuccessful. The

150

certainty that a man means marriage and nothing else may be the magic that brings him to it. Don't take any notice of what we say. Go on, Manila, and marry the gentleman, for I am sure you think, and I am sure he will soon think, he means marriage. If I could see you successful I might be braver myself."

But Manila had stood enough. Her astonishment at the language of aristocrats, the nervous strain of comportment, the doubts that had been thrown on the safety of her future, all this confirmed and heightened the panic in her soul. She had been on show from morning to night; she was dressed to imitate success, but from head to foot nothing belonged to her, not a glass sapphire, not a black satin shoe. She had not about her scanty limbs nor in her borrowed bag a handkerchief that was her own, and picking up a soft cushion of silver tissue she buried her lovely face and wept into its depths.

The duke's daughter came back from the window and looked at her.

"We are all crying," she said. "What a panicky business it is to be a girl!"

"Oh hush!" said Serena taking Manila's hand. "Poor child, yes, she is in the same boat as we are, as I am. What other boat is there to sail in?"

"Well, some people are married," said the duke's daughter. "I, for instance, am at least engaged. Though, heaven knows, if it were to fall through at the last I could never repeat the experience."

"How did it happen?" asked Serena, and Manila lifted her tear-stained face to listen.

"It happened on the golf links," said the duke's daughter, her eyes shining. "That is how Elijah must have felt when he was called up to heaven. A light shone out and a man's voice asked me to marry him, for no reason that I know of in the world. And that is what haunts and alarms me; for where you are engaged for no reason there seems no reason why you should marry."

"Was that the first proposal you ever had?"

152

"When I was nineteen I had four proposals. But it is the old story. At nineteen I remembered who I was and no one seemed brilliant enough. Since then everyone has remembered who I am and no one has been willing to presume on so much brilliance. At nineteen I believed the world was at my feet, and it may have been. But when I ceased to believe it I lost courage and confidence and attraction and power. Humility seems to me no prop for a young woman."

"Manila," said Serena, "you hear that conclusion. Keep your self-confidence (if you really have it!). We are villains to undermine it with our doubts. As for me, humility is the keynote to my character. I cannot uproot it. But I recognize at every fresh adventure its fatal effect upon my fortunes. The image fixed in my mind besets my lovers; and where they should see, and bow before, the empire of my poor beauty, they are aware instead of something which, though it does not expect harm and abuse, is prepared for it; and like terriers they chase

the flying cat solely because it flies. I
have never demanded anything, and I
have never received anything. That,
Manila, is not a position nor a confession
to be proud of."

"You are all preaching at me," said
Manila with a tearful pout. "And I cried
because I was tired. But if you want to
know the truth I was married to Mr.
Simon this morning."

"The great dressmaker!" cried the
duke's daughter. "He is here to-night.
He brought you."

"He brought his wife!" said Manila
with the utmost triumph. "And if a poor
girl like myself can marry so easily it
seems a pity that a great lady like you
should so demean herself in conversation."

"But how wonderful!" said Serena,
with real pleasure. For she was so rare
a creature that she could even sympathise
with success. "Have you been long engaged?"

"I won't tell you anything," replied
Manila fiercely. "I don't believe in such

154

discussions. The affairs of a man and a woman are sacred to themselves. I wouldn't have told you a lie about the gentleman who comes to the showroom only you were so inquisitive. I was brought up to think it rude to ask such questions of strangers."

"Ah," said the duke's daughter, "but there are exceptions. We were in the high realm of Candour."

"I don't know anything about that!" cried Manila, "I only know I don't feel safe. After the way you talk you might be asking a person anything. Why, you all but had the impudence to ask me if I was honest!"

"And are you?" asked Serena.

"Are *you*?" replied Manila in a fury.

"No," said Serena, smiling.

"That is the high realm of which I was speaking," said the duke's daughter gently.

At this moment Mr. Simon walked into the room. He had come to rescue a mannequin who was wasting her sweetness on the desert air, for even the trous-

155

seau of a duke's daughter would not, he felt, when she was marrying a billiard professional, afford him much advantage.

But the voices that greeted him offered him soft congratulations, and he stood amazed in the doorway.

"Your wife has confessed her wedding," said the duke's daughter. "What a wonderful day for both of you!"

"My wife?" enquired Mr. Simon.

"They baited me, Mr. Simon!" cried Manila still astride her indignation. "If this is society I won't come out into it any more. They haven't the morals of poor girls, and they haven't the courage of mice! I said I was married to you because they seem to think I couldn't marry anyone. I'm not afraid of you, Mr. Simon, and if I've got to meet duchesses I'd rather see them cringing in the show-room because they want to buy a dress cheap, than sitting up on high in their own drawing-rooms and talking about their private lives and wanting to know about mine. Mr. Simon, I know you're going to sack me. Well, I give you my resignation, and I feel I should like a change. Mr. Harvey of Nichols has offered me a situation, and though they aren't so classy, it's a shop where there are more home comforts, and I'm not one now for much ambition about high life."

And slipping by Mr. Simon, with tears of desperation on cheeks which had mounted the high flare of courage, she swept into the hall, and whisking up her silk cloak, on out into the night.

"What a young spitfire!" said Mr. Simon, looking after her with admiration. As a Jew he admired moral courage immensely, being the quality he most lacked in himself. "I'm really almost prepared to marry her. But you should know," he went on to the duke's daughter (Serena his sure instinct had in a moment classed as a social nonentity), "that dressmakers never marry their mannequins. You might almost take that as an axiom if ever a girl tells you such a thing again."

"Why not?" asked the duke's daughter. "Artists sometimes marry their models."

157

"Quite different," said Mr. Simon. "Doctors may also marry their patients. But that's quite different too. In both cases they are concerned with the bodies of the young ladies, though only professionally. With the personality of the body I may say. But in my case I'm only concerned with the personality of the covering. I don't want the young person inside to have too much personality. It distracts my vision; it interferes; it gets through the lines of a creation and fuddles my decisions. All that is necessary to me is an exquisite face, a pair of white cotton ankles, and a body so thin and straight that I can make curves on it myself. I don't mind them having brains, a woman's brains. But they mustn't have personality."

"What do you mean by a woman's brains?"

"Well, I like them to follow, you know; follow my meaning. Like a partner following a man's lead at a dance. But I won't have criticism. And I won't have impatience."

158

"It seems to me," said Serena, "that Manila has personality, criticism, and impatience."

"That's why I'm so astonished," said Mr. Simon. "That girl has been a marvel of blankness. The best of my mannequins. The loveliest, the most tireless, and the most imperturbable. I never saw her break out like that before. And now I've lost her. Fancy her having the audacity to turn and hoodwink you like that! And in this house too! Why it's not a thing I would have cared to have done myself. I'll tell you what though, the little spitfire, she'll never make a good mannequin again, now she's broken out, but there's no knowing she might not make a first-rate wife!"

"But I thought your axiom was——" began the duke's daughter. Mr. Simon, however, was gone out into the hall, and into the night—on his mating.

"We have," said Serena, "to-night had a sort of lesson on magic."

"From the lady or from the gentleman?"

"From the lady. Manila is a woman of action, not reflection. I thought her as desolate as she is lovely, but she is far from being in my situation. She is simple and confident; she acts as her character directs. She keeps her flag flying, she will not allow that she is in peril. She has pride and reticence, and even a little mystery. In some compound of these ingredients lies the magic which evokes an honourable intention."

"She has great beauty too."

"I too have great beauty," said Serena indifferently. "And you have birth. That is not the magic. Come, let us go up into the drawing-room, or the countess will send still another messenger to find us."

At midnight Serena's door opened, and her little figure emerged. Wrapped in a dressing gown she sought and found the baize door to the back stairs and ran down the wooden flights to the pantry. There was a slit of light under the door and she tapped.

"Come in," said Martin, who was writing in his diary.

"You are busy?" said Serena timidly.

"I am a little discouraged!" said Martin, and a look almost human settled on his face. "But I do not allow sympathy," he warned her, and as he spoke the look was gone.

When she had told him about her evening and of her conversation with Manila and the duke's daughter, Martin said: "There is no disadvantage like being a woman."

"But Manila has gained a rich husband."

"There may always be a lucky fluke," said Martin. "And what you will find so disheartening is that women do not marry on their merits. But to be practical, and to business, for it is past midnight, and the originality of these gentlemen may as well lead them to get up at six as to stay in bed till twelve. I have found out very little. There is only one manservant between them, and he is now drunk by the fire in the kitchen. To be brief, the

young man whom you allowed to kiss
you——"

"I would have told you," said Serena,
"but how could you know?"

"—is unfortunately for you not very
eligible. Else you would have lost him.
There are several others in a penniless
condition. All the artists and the poets
are married. You will find in life that
all artists and all poets marry before they
are twenty-two. They need comfort and
sympathy earlier than other men, and
are not really fond of independence.
Musicians, on the other hand, prefer living in hotels and are not so drawn to
matrimony. Besides, they work harder.
No, among all those whom the princess
has brought with her there is not one
worth your efforts. And as for Count
Montague, who may be coming if he can
be found, and if he is still in the mood
to join the others, the story goes that he
is enormously rich and very reserved, but
whether he is married I cannot at present
discover.

"Therefore, in order that you may be

clear as to your position, you are at liberty
to kiss all the men in the princess's party,
and in fact all married men and batchelors who are not eligible. Though why
you should have such an inclination is
a puzzle to me, for you are not of an
amorous disposition."

"I am not indeed," said Serena seriously, for nothing hurt her more than
the shadow of such a suggestion. "If I
have any fault it is one of compliance,
any weakness it is the inability to refuse.
I am not vain enough to be flattered, or
foolish enough to mistake a kiss for love,
but alas I am so fatally used to em-
braces, that I never find the heart to refuse what to me is such a trifle and to him
who asks it appears such a real desire."

"Your trouble," said Martin, "is that
you do not want anything very much."

"But I want to get married."

"I ought to have said—that you do not
expect anything very much. But I do not
diagnose, and I do not explain. If I, as
your doctor, could say 'Here is the ail-
ment and here the bottle of medicine,'

163

life would be too simple. You must do your best. I can tell you where you are wrong but not how to be right. I, like the countess, adore success, but for obscurer reasons. There is very little that one can get out of life, but fame, notoriety, position, and wealth are four things that are ridiculously despised by intellectual snobs. As for happiness it is never there when you want it, lovers do not really love, as you have quite justly, but apparently uselessly, discovered, friends are irritated by you even while they love you, and when they are with you they are continually contrasting your achievements and opinions unfavourably with their own. Each creature must prefer itself, or we should die of envy. It is not worth while to be unsuccessful and to console oneself with the pleasures of the spirit, for such pleasures are not always convincing, and what you cannot dangle before your friends does not always exist in your own estimation."

164

"But you yourself, Martin, if those are your beliefs, how are you consoled?"

"Have I griefs?" asked Martin. "And secondly, there is nothing in my position analogous to yours. I am a man, and therefore I cannot gain in marriage. Thirdly, I do not allow you to discuss me."

"It is amazing to me," said Serena, "how much charm I find in someone who speaks so like a schoolmaster."

"I cannot," said Martin, staying her with his hand and rising to terminate the interview, "allow anyone inferior to myself to touch on my character."

IT was on the morrow that Serena came on a woman in the hall, an Amazon of six foot, swathed in soft draperies.

"May I see the Countess Flor di Folio?" asked the woman in the hollow voice of a young male. "I am the secretary of Count Montague D'Costa, who is now staying at the Ritz."

"The countess is out," said Serena, delighted that the count should be found, but distracted by the appearance of his secretary. "Come into this room and wait. You will be warmer."

The secretary preceded Serena into a small room near the hall, and sitting down drew off her gloves and held her hands to the fire. It was a chilly morning and the great hands shone blue and crimson in the blaze. The neck of her soft grey dress was cut low and a male neck of

166

muscles and sinews was exposed, on which lay the trumpery and almost shocking fragility of a gold locket.

"Count Montague missed the boat at Calais?" enquired Serena.

"Yes," said the secretary, "we have only arrived this morning. I wired to the Ritz from Calais and luckily they had rooms for us. Count Montague is now having his bath."

"I think you were expected here," said Serena, "they have been preparing rooms this morning."

"I have come to explain to the Countess Flor di Folio that Count Montague would be delighted if he might dine here whenever he is permitted, but that as he has a great deal of business to settle in connection with his estates he would find it more convenient, and he is sure that the countess too will find it more convenient, if he were to remain for the present at the Ritz. I have also his compliments to give to the princess."

"The princess has gone out with the countess to buy an aquarium," said

167

Serena. "I am sure you must be very tired."

The secretary, for all her appearance of a gaunt bank clerk draped in chiffon, had the gentle gestures of a woman. The sinewy arms emerging from the soft grey frills were folded languidly and hung over her knee. She lifted her face and her feminine and melancholy brown eyes gazed at Serena. She sighed, for something about Serena's beauty caused her to sigh, and lifting her hand she rested her chin and mouth behind its cover as if she had remembered the black down on her upper lip and would like to have hidden it.

"I am tired," she said. "The morning after a journey by night is discouraging."

"Tell me about Count Montague," said Serena, settling comfortably on the sofa.

But at this the secretary grew less languid. Though she experienced the dawning of sympathy for this lovely little creature she was not going to tell her anything about the defenceless, the now nakedly-bathing employer.

168

"He will come himself to pay his call to-day," she said. "I must find out when the countess will be able to receive him."

"Count Montague is more ceremonious than the rest of the princess's party," said Serena.

"Yes," said the secretary, meekly, looking into the flames.

"She loves him," guessed Serena, attracted by the nervous fingers playing with the gold bangle, by a look of contemplative devotion in the poor brown eyes. "Her eyes are the only signals left in her face," thought Serena, "that she was once a woman. Is that what virginity does to the virtuous?" and for a moment panic blew up in her mind like a wind, until she remembered that though a spinster she was not a virgin.

"I have a friend," said Serena, "who insists that it is a great disadvantage to be a woman. Do you find it so in your work?"

"It is like working in chains," the secretary replied at once, as though she had already given the matter much calm

thought. "Our pulling a plough in a
bearing rein. One makes twice the effort
for half the result and a great deal of
energy is wasted. Then there are dis-
tractions, hindrances, and disabilities. It
is all very wasteful."

"You find it so in your work," said
Serena, "but my friend's contention was
that it is even a disadvantage to be *any*
woman."

"A married woman?" asked the secretary in her hollow tones.

"I suppose so," replied Serena. "That
I cannot verify. But it is certainly a
disaster to be single-handed in such a
world as mine."

"It is a subject," said the secretary, "to
which I closed my mind ten years ago."

"Why, what happened to you ten years
ago?" asked Serena.

"I was pulled out of the Seine," said
the secretary.

"Oh——" murmured Serena, appalled.
"And did you go into it on purpose?"

"Yes," said the secretary. "It took a
great deal of reflection, but I had at the

170

time certain difficulties which appeared insoluble."

"And since you were not then to die did you find a solution of the difficulties possible?"

"I did not consider them any more. They no longer appeared important. The creature which they took wet and unrecognisable from the water was in actual fact a corpse. It was the death of a young woman. The being who began life when I came out of hospital was, in all but a physical aspect, a man. And even the physical aspect," said the grim and hollow voice, "has done its best to conform."

"Were you very ill when you jumped into the water?"

"I was excessively well. No one can commit suicide who is not in good health."

"How is that?"

"One may long have been ill with a mental or physical malady, and suicidally inclined. But the act itself will occur on the day when the suicide is at his strongest, when a return of health has given him courage, and a return of spirits the extra energy to perform. Have you never noticed in the accounts in the papers that on the previous night the man who is to commit suicide is at his best, seems in good spirits, and causes no suspicion to his friends? Those spirits are not assumed. It may be that he is in good spirits because he has at last decided—or it may be that his good spirits cause him later to decide. That you can only tell by the date and hour of his preparations, should there be a clue to them afterwards."

"And you, sitting before me, have gone through all this?"

"What I was," went on the secretary, unheeding, "I can tell you quite plainly, without emotion, for since then I have not only changed my life, shifted my hopes, avoided old despairs, planted new ambitions, but I have all but changed my sex."

"It was a man who caused you such unhappiness?"

"No," came the answer; "unhappily, unhappily I cannot boast that it was. It might have been his utter absence. I found that I had a nature which at every turn was thwarted by my lack of beauty. My inclinations were entirely feminine. My aspect was entirely forbidding. My shyness found expression in ferocity. Without any foundations for such a fancy, I dreamed of, lived for, marriage. It was my prayer at night, my morning thought, my obsession in the streets and at my work. Yet men whom I tried to attract imagined from my manner that I was repelling them." She paused, but Serena did not speak. "Never to get an instant's satisfaction out of the looking glass——" went on the secretary, her eyes on Serena's golden head. "To turn this way and that, to catch one's image by surprise. Never to get one gleam of beauty! I starved myself to buy face creams, hair tonics, dyes, hats, and silk blouses. Yet I never have seen in any man's eyes one look of admiration. It was not to be expected.

173

"Full of rage and misery I lived in this way until I was twenty-nine.

"When I realised that all I could do with my life was to make enough money in order to put bread and meat into my mouth that I might continue to live, then I decided that to follow this narrow occupation of self-sustenance for another thirty or forty years was unworthy of a human being meant for other pleasures. In short it was unbearable."

"In all that time were you never in love yourself with anyone?"

"I didn't want love," said the secretary. "I didn't want pain. I wanted marriage. I could not respect myself without it."

"So then you decided——" said Serena waveringly.

"Well then, since to live a woman's life was my only desire, one which I could not subdue, and which no man could be expected to satisfy, I said to the obsession, to the young woman within me, 'You cannot live, so you had better die.' But she had got into my head and into my

174

bones and into my movements and I could not do anything with her. So finally I said, 'Well, let the whole thing go, flesh and bones and all.' But after all it was the obsession that was drowned and the flesh and bones were saved. When I woke up in the hospital the young woman was gone. I had not a worry, I had not an impulse. What a resurrection! I lay in bed for weeks and weeks and resolved to fill the young woman's place with a male personality. I watched the nuns, and thought of them ▮▮▮women, and though I could not ▮▮▮ desire, I achieved contempt. I ▮▮▮ to get men's clothes and wear them. When the doctor came I watched his mannerisms, tried to get into his mind and see how it worked, and I found that I could watch him without a care as to my effect upon him. Oh, the young woman was gone, very completely! Even the looking glass showed me that. It was a grim face, but I did not mind its grimness. I got up, left the hospital, and set

175

about getting work. I have been con-
tented ever since."

"And did you dress as a man?"

"For a time," said the secretary, dream-
ily. "It was a great help at first. But
afterwards I grew so secure of male outlook that I could afford to do without
men's clothes. And I have perhaps just
a lingering weakness left in all the
change——" She smoothed her grey
chiffon dress. "I kept my trinkets, the
things I had bought when the young
woman lived. They were like the tres-
ured oddments of a wretched sister
I like to buy women's stuffs now
to see them by the yard in the
think of myself as a man who has
ness for silks. But I dress to please myself," she said with a touch of defiance,
"and no one else!"

Into Serena's mind there leapt full-
blown the idea, "It's all a lie. Or it has
all broken down. She is in love again."

The door opened and the countess came
in, followed by four men carrying an

176

enormous case shielded with canvas and roped round its sides.

"Put it down here," said the countess excitedly, and drew four chairs together in a square. Behind her came the princess in a battered hat of gold lace trellis-work and an enormous bunch of violets under her chin.

"Shaftesbury Avenue!" she cried gaily to Serena, "What a place to shop. It's the nearest thing to the Galeries Lafayette."

The men lowered the case on to the chairs, undid the rope and drew off the canvas.

"Shall I get the buckets, m'm?" said the foreman.

"Get them quickly."

The countess knelt down by the great glass cage that had been revealed.

"There is a crack here. No, it's a mark on the glass. If we are going to fill it now where shall we put it?"

"This is an excellent little room," said the princess vaguely, looking the room up

and down as though she were giving it
her attention.

The aquarium was placed in the window, and the men returned with four
buckets, each covered with greased paper
and tied down like the lid of a jam pot.
Tearing off the paper lids, and opening
the sliding roof of the aquarium, they
tipped the buckets carefully, and out the
bright fishes flashed. Moss and sand and
fishes and salt water fought and swam in
a haze, and soon, the sand sinking, and
the moss floating, the fish fastened their
gaping snouts to the wall of glass like
travellers bewitched by a spirit resis-
tance in the midst of a journey.

Serena drew Flor's attention to the secretary.

"Count Montague has turned up," said
the princess.

The secretary gave her message.

"Oh he must come to-night," said Flor.
"Can he come to-night?"

"He will be delighted." And picking
up a little sateen umbrella with a gilt
handle the secretary gathered her frills
about her and disappeared.

178

CHAPTER IX

THE princess spoke of the glamour and
the riches of Count Montague, the countess did not contradict her, and Serena,
who was prepared for anything, and believed what she was told, who knew no
other society than the countess's world,
would not have thought it strange if the
King of England had dined at the countess's table.

If she had allowed her dreams to dwell
anywhere they would have dwelt all day
on the young man who was expected in
the evening. But she had no dreams.

"Is he come?" she said to Martin in the
hall, as she passed, dressed, into the drawing-room. He nodded.

"Another batchelor," she was inclined
to add a little wearily, "another opportunity."

Alone, within the drawing-room, the

illustrious Portuguese was leaning against the mantelpiece, an emerald on either hand, and thoughtfully manicuring his brilliant nails.

As she entered he turned on her a sloe-black look of admiration, but said not a word. And Serena, who had never found conversation a necessity, was equally content to return his look with her own beautiful response. This idyll, so effortless and pleasant, was interrupted by the arrival of the countess, not, however, before Serena had whispered to herself with the certainty born of long and delightful experience, "In another moment he would have kissed me."

The room was filled with guests, the countess swept them in to dinner, and placed Count Montague upon her right. But the evening was not far advanced before it became apparent that he had very little conversation. Behind his gold pince-nez his eyes were blackly brilliant, his teeth and his smile flashed constantly in a readiness to please, and it was obvious that he did not understand a quarter of what was said to him, and to what he understood he could not always discover a reliable reply. The countess, who was no snob, having paid deference to Count Montague's reputation, could no longer endure his intolerable English, and the young man sat, without embarrassment, in a dignified and preoccupied isolation.

But to Serena, who did not deal in conversation, who did not notice externals, who took the word of Martin, or the word of the countess, who saw charm in any man who would make love to her, and had only regretfully learnt that kindness did not shine in every smile—to Serena the silence into which he gradually sank amid the hubbub and the brilliance of the countess's surroundings only added to his charm, and to the moments when she could subject herself to his admiring examination.

It was not admiration which was so delightful to her, for she was unchangeably humble, but a look of conquest was a wine that she could not withstand, and

a question in a man's eye was a question
to which she always answered "yes." In
vain did Martin frown at her ravished
looks, in vain he picked up her napkin,
filled her glass and whispered icy cau-
tions in her ear. Then when he saw that
what he said was useless, to a man of his
pride further expostulation was impossible, and with contempt he left her to her
glances and their replies.

Serena, for the hundredth time since
she had been under the countess's roof,
had forgotten her primary design. Marriage—with so brilliant a creature, with
a rich young man who wore such emeralds, with a foreigner of romantic family
and glorious fortune, such a word was
frightened out of her head. No, but *admiration* she could look for from kings,
desire was not out of place in any man's
eyes, and sinking back into the unassum-
ing rôle which she had always played, she
forgot her penniless pockets, the countess's commands, the advice of Martin,
the reason, the very reason for which she
wore the green taffeta dress.

For Serena, having no future, could never remember it. To give way to the present was all her instinct. And the shine in the satin eye of this stranger, made with its demand on her, all her horizon. She was in no misapprehension concerning that demand. She knew its origin, its nature, and its goal, and while she would have agreed with Martin and with the countess about the perishable nature of blonde beauty and the danger of her spinstered position, she was aware that even though she gave up a distant kingdom to reply yet her nature would dictate her mesmerised responses to any man who chose to ask her the mischievous and enamoured question.

And to this she was never driven by love or by desire, but solely because of her impulse towards the luxury of acceptance.

Martin, who had taken a certain interest in her, could hardly be said to be nervous about his own position. He would not allow that any creature alive could make demands upon him, but partly because he saw himself as the dark god who drove the chariot of her fortunes, partly because he was a tiresome meddler, and partly because he had in him something tyrannical and yet spinsterish which expected (though he should have known better) that life would dovetail, he demanded and desired and even schemed for her marriage. Any weakness, any display of her lamentable nature, infuriated him. He knew, better than she in her absurd humility, that even Portuguese counts can be caught in marriage. From his own fund of curious knowledge he had ascertained, as he bent over with the vegetable dishes, that the young man's emeralds were not glass. He saw, with a cold eye, that the wastrel was looking her loveliest, and that Count Montague had observed it; but when he saw her bury her glances in his looks of admiration, even as she buried her chances of a fortune, he felt a venomous disillusion take hold of him and he muttered, "It is my misfortune that I can never find any creature entirely worthy

184

of my interest." But Serena, wasteful and uncalculating, was preserved from the clearer expression of her weakness. Throughout the evening, even in the drawing-room, when guest after guest battled with the count's English, failed, and passed him on to another, Serena could not contrive to find herself by his side. Though for that matter she did not scheme in any way, for if she had a rule of conduct it was to remain passive upon the brink of adventure, and to let the tide of approaching seduction sweep over her upon its own impetus.

That he made no effort to approach her did at least excite her wonderment. "But it is true," she murmured, "that men's actions are incalculable. One does not know what moves or what restrains them, nor what motives succeed each other across the mind. Though it amused him to admire me over a dinner table, he may now feel that his eyes have said too much, and that his words, on a nearer approach, are not prepared to keep pace with them. He is afraid to compromise himself."

"How restful," she thought with a sigh, "is the attitude of married men. They approach without fear, have no need to be soothed and reassured, are not for ever, like these batchelors, starting back in restless and fatiguing distrust." And she felt towards Count Montague like someone who wishes to stroke a wild animal, to appease its fright, to calm it, and assure it no harm and no capture is intended.

The evening passed, and completed her preservation. Not once did she have an opportunity of showing Count Montague how completely she was at his mercy. As he said good-bye to the countess his eye wandered, and again Serena could believe that his admiration was undiminished, and though they had not said a word to each other she had no doubt that once alone they would find the perfect expression of their mutual comprehension.

Freed, however, from the invitation of his eye, she shook off her foolish intoxication.

"How idle," she thought, "for me to linger in such a house as this, and with such hopeless pretensions. Is it not vexing that though I dress each night for marriage, I am perpetually prepared to undress for other reasons. I am far from disillusion but it cannot be denied that the days are passing, that no proposal has come near me, and that with such a nature as mine it is only a miracle that can get me to the altar."

Three days went by and Count Montague did not appear.

"He is not well," said the secretary who came to make his excuses.

"We will come and see him," said Flor, noting it in her book among her day's engagements.

But the secretary's long features lengthened, and she glanced suspiciously at Serena.

"He is not well enough to receive visitors," she insisted.

"So ill as that?" asked the countess coldly, glancing at her with disbelief.

The woman set her mouth. "He is not

himself. When he is ill he is better quite alone."

"Do you nurse him then?" pursued the countess.

"Yes," replied the secretary squarely. Serena's blue eyes meeting the melancholy brown eyes received a look of despair. It was a challenge to her curiosity, and she said, "I will walk back part of the way with you to your hotel."

The secretary nodded.

Out in the sunshine Serena realised that they had not far to walk.

"Come into the Park," she suggested, and again the secretary acquiesced.

But when they sat on a seat in the park the lank woman had nothing to say, and leaning on her inadequate sunshade she stared at the ground.

"You have been up all night," said Serena. "You are tired. Is he so ill?"

"I have been up all night," said the expressionless voice. "He is not ill at all."

"You mean there is nothing the matter with him?"

"Have you made love to him?" groaned the secretary. "He says he is in love with you."

Serena received this with her customary humility—as one to whom nothing is a surprise and nothing to her credit.

"I have not yet spoken to him," she replied. And at that there was a silence, of disbelief on the part of the secretary, of reflection on the part of Serena.

"I have never felt love. Like you I am only concerned with marriage," continued Serena. "I feel affection. I am ready to do a good turn to another. I do not hurt, or damage, or desire. No, I have never felt love, the extraordinary emotion which does not bring with it one spark of kindness, carries no gifts in its hand, springs up in a night and dies down at a request. If your count feels any flame which I have kindled you are right to say, 'He is in love with you!' But if he would *marry* me I would not say, 'He is in love with me,' but, joyfully, 'He is as I am. He feels affection. He wants my happiness. He wants my friendship.'

"But your count—no! For beautiful as I am, I am as you were. No one wants to marry me, and your count, like every other man who has ever come near me, if he wants anything at all, wants no more than to make me his mistress."

The secretary looked at her in surprise, and though about to speak she suppressed the impulse and continued silent.

"I have had experiences," continued Serena placidly, "which would cure the most expectant woman. I carry with me a nature which is my perpetual pitfall.

"I am not, as you were, unhappy, proud, and unable to submit myself. On the contrary my very docility is in turn the salvation of my content and the enemy of my fortunes, but I was not meant for a life in which adventure must be turned to profitable account. The little I am able to draw from the progress of my misfortunes is gentle sustenance for my private reflections. I am not bitter, I am disillusioned, but I must own that I have come to the conclusion that my own heart is kinder than the heart of any man, and that there are things that I would do for others that they will not do for me."

The secretary remained silent for a moment.

"I thought," she said at last in a peculiar tone, "that I ought to warn you. I did not know that anyone so young and beautiful could be so completely on her guard. Count Montague has expressed his admiration of you. Even to me, his secretary, he does not hesitate to discuss you. Although I am devoted to his interests I must tell you as a woman that he has indeed" (she smiled sardonically) "a black side. He is licentious and unruly. Where his passions are concerned he is unsafe. The blood of many nations is in his veins, and the combination in his case is such that it drives him mad upon occasion. This is the secret of his three days' absence. Knowing him as I do, and armed as I was when I was engaged as his secretary by the advice of his relations, I have managed to control him, soothe him, and check his wish to see you. I could not," continued the secretary, warming to her story and looking almost happy, "forget your frailty, your delicacy of feature, your kindness to me. I could not unloose on you this nightmare of wild passion. You are indeed right. Marriage is the last subject of his thoughts. He wished of course to make you his mistress, and had he done so (you would naturally have tried to withstand him), but had he done so——" (she paused, and leaning nearer to the fascinated Serena, she whispered):

"There have been two former scandals in his life, and of such magnitude and horror that it was only by the wealth and intrigue of his family that he has been kept out of the police court. In both cases the victim——"

"Died!" gasped Serena.

"Strangled," replied the secretary with a horrible look of malice.

"Does the princess know this?" asked Serena.

"You must not tell her."

"But she is in danger! For from what

she openly acknowledges she makes continual attempts upon his nature."

"She is utterly without attraction for him," replied the secretary, her lips curling with contempt. "Count Montague's nature is inflamed in a second or never at all. The princess is as safe with him as his horse or his dog. But you, you, such a face as yours must never look at his again! While he is here in London you must escape him. Can you not go to relatives? For I cannot control him for ever and he will soon insist on visiting the countess's house again, and on searching for you. He has only consented to remain at the Ritz these three days because he happened to cut himself while shaving, and as he is very vain I played upon his vanity and told him that the cut would displease and disgust you. Now it is almost healed, and the sun is shining. Everything will tempt him to go out. He is on fire to find you again."

"But you have told the countess that he is ill."

"His English is so difficult and she is
193

such a poor listener that they will hardly communicate. Besides, once an invalid is well again no one troubles to discuss his illness."

"I don't want to die," said Serena at last. "But I have nowhere to go, and besides that I cannot feel very alarmed. I have been the object of the whims and desires of a great many people, but I have never witnessed in another creature such a passion as you describe. I cannot believe that anything so definite as death is in store for me, and at all events when I see him I shall have the protection of the countess's friends and servants about me. I cannot go away, for if I leave the countess it is very doubtful whether she will allow me to return.

"If the count's love incites him even to murder it bears out what I believe, that love is an evil and unkind emotion and that so long as I am weak enough to listen to it I shall get no particular security out of life."

"You are mad," said the secretary in a flat and despairing voice. And seeming

194

to fall into a deep reflection she remained silent while Serena sat attentively beside her.

When she rose the secretary's tears were falling down her face, and her bony hand was clenched over the handle of her sunshade. "I have warned you; you must do your best," she said, and added, "So must I."

Serena walked back to Berkeley Square. On her way she was followed by a young man in a bowler hat. As such a thing had not happened to her for several weeks it served to lighten and distract her spirits, but when she was in sight of the countess's door she saw the back of the Jew to whom she owed eighty pounds. The young man in the bowler hat ceased to be a comfort to her. "So early in the morning!" she thought. "How horrible to meet misfortune before luncheon. Alas Martin will be cleaning his gold plate and there will be no one better than a footman to protect me." For she knew that the countess had not gone out and that there was every likelihood that the

Jew would be shown directly into her boudoir.

The young man who followed her, noting her preoccupied air, and seeing from her manner that she had more important business that morning in her mind, lifted his hat and disappeared down a side street.

Serena, willing to be distracted from the predicament ahead of her by any passing incident, noticed his disappearance with regret.

"How vagrant and light as thistle-down," she thought, standing still in the sunlight, "how idle, and easily scared are the fancies of men who follow women in the street! They are not hunters, but a roaming, poaching brotherhood, ready to fly at a frown, to scuttle at the shrug of an indifferent shoulder."

It was late spring. The coloured awnings were out already for the summer.

"Soon," thought Serena, facing the door, "my fur cape will be no use to me. Also my silver hat is tarnished, the Jew

196

is with the countess, and this is an end to my opportunities."

She mounted the steps and rang the bell.

It was Martin, not a footman, who opened the door.

"Heaven is not kind to you, Serena," he said. "My poor child, you have no luck. I warned you, I think, to make hay while the sun of the countess's favour shone. At this moment of the morning it is also for you sunset." He pointed to the closed door of the boudoir, from behind which came voices.

"Will she send me away?" murmured Serena, turning pale.

"The countess," said Martin, "is not very original. She may take the violent fancies of a child, but she has also its directness. She has few subtleties, she remains in character, and what one might expect her to do she very often does. If it were the princess the very fact of your debt might amuse her, for she is poor and her life is spent upon margins, but the countess, being rich, has a peculiar

197

horror of debt, and though she is often delighted by the triumphant oddities of other people, she is never amused by want of success. Your beauty in this house has been remarked but it has never produced results, and I would not at this moment give a penny for your chance of remaining here."

"Are you not sorry for me, Martin?"

"No," replied the cruel butler, "I am more sorry for my own disappointment. I, like the countess, specialise in results, and I do not like my pottery to break. You trifle with success, you are without ambition—lovely as you are and armed with such a weapon it is discouraging that only the merest accident can come between you and failure."

"You are inhuman," cried Serena, bursting into tears. "I would marry anyone, *anyone* who would ask me!"

"Anyone?"

"Anyone!" sobbed Serena, now at the end of her courage.

"Well," said Martin as he left her, "that is something. If I bully you am I

not at the same time your best friend?
Who but I would take the trouble to
bring you to the proper frame of mind
for a beautiful and friendless young woman!"

The door of the boudoir opened and
the Jew came out. Seeing his victim already in tears before he was quite beyond
her reproaches, he snatched up his hat
and hurried to the front door. The countess, who had followed him into the hall,
now called Serena into the boudoir.

The interview was terrible. Disliking
tears or any sign of weakness the countess
warmed to her task.

"When I offered you the pleasures of
my house and my world," she finished, "I
did not mean that you should occupy my
mind or my time. My house and my life
are too full to allow me to give the hours
to your problem that it needs. You will
find in life that people do not do more
than offer you a passing chance. They
may be willing to give money but they
will not give you their time. You are
beautiful, and I adore beauty. But you

are a fool and that is the end of it. You
will never marry. If you are not convinced of that peril I will bring it home
to you. You will leave me to-night.

"Meanwhile for the rest of the day
you may enjoy yourself," said the countess
grimly. "There is a luncheon party.
You may behave like the daughter of the
house; no one will frown at you, no one
will know that you are going. Do what
you like, try what you can. But when
the evening comes leave me without saying good-bye. I do not dislike gratitude
but I have enough sense to know that you
will not thank me for the opportunities
which I have given you, but only dislike
me for the opportunities which I have
withdrawn."

"And gratitude," wept Serena, unable
though in despair to resist a reflection,
"is, even at its purest, a mixed emotion."

"You may take," said her benefactress,
rising to end the conversation, "the silver
hat which I gave you. It is tarnished,
but it suits you. The fur cape too will
keep you warm and I should like you to

have it. But the green taffeta dress which you wore last night will be useless to you when you no longer mix in society. Leave it behind for I may find a use for it."

With that she was gone and Serena left alone upon the sofa.

Serena dried her eyes, and sat without moving in unhappy thought. She reviewed her life in the house which she was leaving, and considered how difficult it is to be a benefactress, how difficult to be a protégée; how whimsical the countess's affection for her, how whimsical her dislike.

"From the moment that she began to tire of me," she reflected, "she began to think more and more of the service she was doing me. From the moment of her change of feeling how quickly she flew to extremes against me." She concluded that where affection is given without intimacy anything may curdle it in a moment.

"She is right," she thought, "when she said that I should feel more resentment at my dismissal than gratitude for my adoption. I also feel more regret at losing the green taffeta dress than relief at keeping the hat and the cape. There is one thing only that consoles me in all this, and that is a faint, evaporating consolation; my heart at least is superior to hers, for I would not in her place have behaved so coldly to another. And yet perhaps, having never been rich, I do not know how difficult it is to give." Resting her head in her hands she began to wonder what she would now do with her future.

The door opened and the footman showed in Count Montague D'Costa.

The door closed. He crossed the room and sat down beside her. She was alone with a monster, silent, sinister, and on fire with love.

IT was not two hours since the secretary had warned Serena of Count Montague's horrible passion for her, of his distressing tendencies and his mysterious past.

"If I am strangled," thought Serena, her head still leaning in her hands, "the countess will be convinced that at least one of her young men has admired me. If I am half strangled and rescued (there are the servants), I shall attain the notoriety of which Martin thinks so much. If, without strangling me, he merely makes love to me I may have found at the last moment a wealthy protector. It is a good thing to hope, as Martin is so fond of saying, and though I have never yet found a man who was willing in any way to provide for me, I too am no cynic. I like to believe in the future."

And while she thus reflected, she did

not look to left or right, but through her
fingers at the floor.

It is a good thing to hope. Count
Montague, rising, leaned over her bent
head. While she waited for the crack-
ling of the flame which she had kindled,
while she waited for the grip of passion
at her throat, Count Montague was trans-
lating his thoughts into sentences—and
while her eyes and face were hidden she
heard above her the healing words of
enamoured respect, the slow phrasing of
the Impossible Proposition.

Dizzily she waited for him to recant
them, explain them, twist them to some
darker end. He took her hand.

She had heard his few words, she knew
what they meant: a man young and rich
had proposed to her. Was it possible?
She thought of the duke's daughter, of
Manila. Yes, to both this enchanted
accident had occurred.

"Do you love me?" he stammered.

She had no answer on her tongue, and
nothing more radiant than determination

in her heart. For a moment she was
silent that she might make no mistake.

"I am one of those who can transfigure
a fellow creature!" and her eyes shed the
strangest tears in the moment of triumph,
since she could find no such miracle on
earth for herself.

Now he too was silent, waiting for an
answer. She did not know what to reply.
She dared not grow eager. She knew
that the poison in her eyes dissolved
resolution and honour in men. She
dared not raise them. She gave him her
dumb hands; yet remembering that even
they had their language she forbade them
to answer his pressure. Slipping to her
knees she let fall her head upon the sofa
and knelt before a rich and honourable
young man.

Serena did not know why he had proposed to her, nor could she guess in what
light she appeared to him. Whether in
his foreignness he supposed her to be of
birth and society, whether, groping
among those complicated layers of a
world strange to him he supposed her to

be of the best, whether after all he loved
her; at any rate from his lips, in stumb-
ling speech, had come a firm determined
offer. Serena, the waif, at the black moment of her despair, had landed a count.

Still she did not speak. Out of his
pocket he drew a ring. She gazed at its
monstrous pebble, and her left hand
fluttered up towards him. Chafing her
skin with its exquisite bulk she felt an
emerald that had cost thousands on her
hand.

Breaking into his own language he
now began to speak to her volubly. She
understood well that she was the re-
cipient of love. He caught her to him,
he covered her with kisses: here, though
on her own ground, and knowing her
part, she forbore to offer the gestures of
love. He murmured to her in English,
"I adorate you!" and she was silent with
triumph, silent with that silence, too,
which has nothing to say.

The door burst open, and Flor stood
on the threshold. Serena lifted her
emerald.

"He has asked me to marry him. He has asked me to be his wife." The words, spoken aloud, were fantastic. Might not the heavens thunder denial?

Martin, behind Flor, was watching from the hall. Serena, her other hand on the arm of her deliverer, humble and giddy, looked up and listened for corroboration.

She had done what they asked of her, she had won, she had saved her footing as she fell, she had caught a friendly hand, a golden hand.

"Is it true?" asked the countess of the count.

He guessed at her meaning.

"We will marry," he said, smiling at his beloved.

"Then it is wonderful, wonderful!" cried Flor with her child's delight. She saw herself a moulder of destiny. Catching the young man's hands she congratulated him, lent forward and kissed him, saying, "You have got a treasure, a beautiful wife. You have stolen my jewel, but I forgive you!"

Dimly now the words of praise and congratulation entered Serena's mind. The overthrow of her misfortunes bewildered her. Her relations with the countess improved before her eyes. Smiles, and the warmest atmosphere, were renewed. She sank down upon the sofa, her face pale.

"She loves you already," said the countess ecstatically to Count Montague. "See how happy you have made her look!" Count Montague, at a loss for more words, wrung the countess's hand. Martin came forward and whispered something.

The countess turned to him.

"There is time," said Martin in a low voice, "to catch the evening papers."

"But I ought to have his authority," said the countess dubiously.

"It must not be an official announcement," said Martin, "but a well-founded rumour."

"Publicity!" said the countess with determination.

Martin withdrew. A footman announced the forerunners of a luncheon party, who, arriving, found themselves in the presence of romance. They appeared delighted, and said all that was suitable, whispering among themselves, "Who is it? Who is he? Is it a good marriage? I never heard of either before."

The countess was pleased with her protégée and the guests accustomed to her toys, so that between her garrulous excitement and their complaisance the marriage was lifted sky-high; and Serena, who believed all that she was told, realised that her feat was as dazzling as she had imagined. She expanded under that shower of counterfeit blessings, she felt the invisible roses and rice.

The photographers, assembled by Martin, were in the hall as they came out from luncheon. Serena paused, her hand on her lover's arm, and smiling faintly she realised that every participator in the knowledge of her engagement made her triumph more secure.

Indeed now she would have been no

longer surprised to find herself married before evening.

So the day proceeded, and not for a moment was either Serena or her count allowed to feel a reaction. He was torn from her on a hundred excuses. Sending for his secretary he explained to her his good fortune, and made her understand that she must see to the hiring of a car for his fiancée. The secretary sat down at a table by the telephone, and collecting her pen and papers about her she wrote and telephoned at the bidding of the countess and the princess.

"Why do you sit with your back to me?" complained Flor as she dictated a paragraph for a newspaper.

"That the light may come over my left shoulder," replied the secretary obstinately, without moving. Her great hand poured out the capering shorthand, and her long face hung in shadow as she listened for the first time to the details, the arrangements, the paraphernalia of engagement.

210

Serena paused in the doorway when she saw her thus at work.

"Go away, my child," said the countess glancing over her shoulder, "we are busy."

And Serena was glad to escape from the sight of the ambiguous male engaged on such a business.

One moment she was filled with a sense of her own escape; another with a sense of Count Montague's kindness.

"Not a word, not a breath of that," said Martin tyrannically, when she found herself for a second alone with him. "We do not know precisely, the countess and I, why he is marrying you. It seems as though it were in mistake, in error. A breath, a whisper, a look, may make him aware before the wedding day *whose* charity is being dispensed and where the suppliant kneels."

"Then am I to be married soon?"

"Immediately, instantly," replied Martin. "It is as well to be married before one is deserted."

"But will he consent?"

"The countess will see to that. He respects her position and believes in her advice."

"Is it possible," brooded Serena, "that I am marrying a man with whom I can hardly communicate?"

"Thank God for that," replied Martin, "else long ere this, my poor child, you would have communicated the truth."

By tea time the penniless girl wore pearls on her neck.

After tea Martin brought her a pile of folded papers.

"Your photograph is in seven of them," he pointed out. "You have an emerald on your finger—and yesterday you had nothing."

Serena, listening, felt the fragility of her success, and her heart all but stopped beating.

"Shall I ever get to the wedding day? Will he?"

"You have this emerald and his pearls," replied her adviser. "If he fails you keep those."

In the evening she wore a mauve dress

which the countess had bought her, and Count Montague's orchids were at her waist.

"Are you happy?" asked Martin, as she was about to end her day and go to bed.

"I have almost ceased to be happy," she said, "or grateful, or triumphant; even the sense of wonder is leaving me, even the sense of my past."

"That is life," said Martin. "You cannot taste anything for long."

In the morning Serena, who had no friends, was astonished to find a letter upon her tray.

"I tried to withstand you," wrote the secretary, "but I could not. As you must have guessed, the young woman I thought was drowned has come back, and *this* time we go to the bottom of the Thames together."

And such was the secretary's awful determination this time to accompany the tormentor within her that her body when recovered was found to be weighted with lead.

213

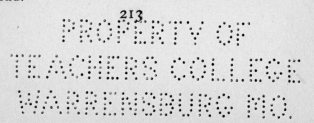

The incident dimmed for a moment the radiance of the engagement.

"Montague has decided," said Flor, while choosing a wreath for the secretary's funeral, "that only a few of his relations should be invited for the wedding."

"If I may stay a little longer," said the princess, who hoped that amorous impatience in the count would weaken his general austerity, "I will empty your house of my young men and send them back to Paris. You will have room then for Montague's relations."

"It is bourgeois to condemn suicide," said Flor, as her choice settled upon red roses. "Write your name on this card, Serena."

Serena was thinking of the secretary.

"Soldiers of fortune," she murmured as she bent over the card, "disheartened campaigners. Yesterday, each in the same pass, we talked under a tree. I, with my beauty which was no use to me, she with a strength of mind which had failed her. To-day she is dead, and I am to be married. Well, she has done what

214

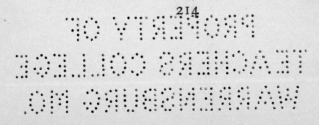

I could not, and I what, after all, she could never have expected to do."

Serena's world clustered close round her. She was never alone for a moment, never idle, never at a standstill. It was as though Flor and her friends had taken her by the hands and run with her towards the date that was fixed.

"An engagement," thought Serena, as she sailed from moment to moment like a ship with a full breeze, "is first made by a miracle, but once made how comfortably, how irreparably it is confirmed by the spectators." She was thankful for such energetic confirmations, and she blessed the worldly and acquainted spirit of the countess.

Lists of the guests were made, Count Montague's relations were invited, the day approached. Serena had no money for a trousseau, but Flor gave her ten yards of white satin and some orange blossom.

"And all I shall need is my wedding dress and a nightgown," reasoned Serena, "for after that it seems I can buy up all Paris."

"If I knew why he is marrying me," she said to Martin, "I should feel safer. Why do you think he is marrying me?"

"God knows," Martin replied.

But for once she did not listen to his answers. If she asked him questions now it was only to calm herself as she flew towards marriage, along the path of a bride.

CHAPTER XI

It was the wedding eve.

All was in readiness for the relations of the bridegroom. In the great ballroom the chairs were drawn back against the walls for the morrow, and at the far end a small baize table held the wedding presents. One branch of the candelabra was turned on; its gloomy light travelling a little way along the parquet floor.

On the baize table lay the odds and ends that Serena's personality had attracted to her. A pen-wiper and a blotter from a banker, a cut-glass dish from Lord Ivor Cream, a seal-dyed coney fur-coat from the countess, and nothing from the offended Sir Verilees. Her mother sent her love and a garnet bangle. Martin's advice could not be exhibited. But the display on the green baize table was too affecting to be contemplated; it should be remembered that those who socially aspire aim at living like cut flowers in water, and must barter their roots for the luxury of a rarer life.

Upstairs in every guest room the fires were burning brightly. The footmen were clustered in the hall, the maids hung about at the head of the staircase, the cars had gone to the station.

"Rest, my child," said the countess to Serena. "Lie on your bed and close your eyes. You will need all your beauty for the evening."

"How pleasant," yawned Serena as she went upstairs, "is popularity. Poverty and failure produce no goodwill, but with a little triumph, a little success, one can purchase something very like kindness."

Obediently she lay down on her bed and closed her eyes, and hearing the parrots in the yard below she remembered the day when she had arrived.

"The fortunes of a young woman are the most hazardous in the world," she reflected. "A man who makes money

takes many years to make it, and even
the few who inherit accidentally go many
months before they can touch their in-
heritance. But every young woman born
on this earth may by chance find herself,
at a word from a stranger, transplanted,
transported, ruined, or offered a fortune.
It is possible at a bound, to become the
wife of a convict; a commoner has been
known to become the wife of a king: we
find our way, like the changing penny,
into the most astonishing pockets, and
life may hold for us anything or nothing,
and that is the bitterness of the years between twenty and thirty. Little can be
got by one's own efforts, and nothing
by one's merits, and at any moment, and
for no reason, a man may hold out his
hand and invite us to share his glory.

"It is strange how securely my engagement surrounds me. Like a cloak for
warmth, like an armour against disdain.
I can no longer believe that I could ever
have been in peril." Prepared for happiness and unresentful towards past ad-
versity, she fell asleep.

She was awakened by the sound of her door softly opened, and Martin stood by her bedside.

"They have come," said Martin, and he began to laugh.

She started up, and, struck by a look in his eyes, turned pale. "Is anything the matter? Do they want to stop the marriage?"

"On the contrary," said Martin, "I should think they are delighted. It seems you are a catch, my child."

"Something has happened!"

"They are in their bedrooms and the maids are waiting on them."

"Something has happened!"

"Have I not given you," mocked Martin, "a husband!"

"You?"

"Did I not bring you to the proper frame of mind? Did I not prepare the soil on which the seed of that brilliant offer was dropped?"

"Ah, Martin, Martin, I would have taken anyone. You are keeping something from me."

Steps sounded on the stair. Martin slipped behind the door. Through its narrow opening Serena saw the countess go by with flushed face and preoccupied eye.

"She will want me," said Martin. "When she gets to her bedroom she will ring for me."

"Martin——"

"Hush," said Martin, "I will admit that there is something a little unusual, a little disappointing about your new relations. Even the countess as you saw has had a shock. But she is a woman of courage, and I am a friend who believes in marriage and looks after your interests. I have come to give you my blessing."

Still without words and pale, she stared at him.

"Say 'thank-you' to my blessing," he insisted.

"If I am to be married—to be married," she said, "I say it in my heart."

"Your heart is no temple," laughed Martin, passing through the door. "I would rather you said it in words."

Upstairs in her bedroom the countess reflected by her window. She had come to a decision. The marriage must go on. She had had a shock, but she was not a woman of prejudices. It was better than no marriage at all. The reporters when they came might have the sense to say little about it; on the other hand, if they grasped its salient feature she would get a cynical credit from this sensational union.

She did not ring for Martin but she used the house telephone.

"Dinner at half-past eight," she said firmly, "and if the florists are still open, ring them up and remind them about the bay trees for the church."

"Formidable and unscrupulous woman," thought Martin. But it was only what he had expected.

Sick, apprehensive, hoping, fearing, with trembling fingers and trembling haste, Serena dressed and crept downstairs.

Taking her little bride from the stairs the countess smoothed her hair, kissed her, and led her forwards. Reassured and smiling, Serena faced the room ahead of her, where through the open door she saw the guests assembled. Montague, waiting by the door, came to her side. Happily the simplest exercise book supplied the necessary words of introduction.

"My aunt," he said, as they entered the drawing-room together. "My uncle, my cousin, my second cousin, my sister, my niece."

Mestizos, half-breeds, dressed by Drécol, young men with the lithe bodies of leopards and eyes like sloes, pressed eagerly round her; light voices, fluttering, sweet, and melancholy, filled the room. As Serena moved forward with her lover, the bridegroom's family murmured delightedly, and women with marvellous figures, took her hand in their long-gloved fingers, or stooped and kissed her, according to their relationship.

Serena, relieved and innocent, was warmed by the admiration in their agate eyes. Their smiling mouths, painted the colour of fresh salmon, welcomed and adored her.

"Which is your mother, Montague?" she whispered.

"My mother could not come," he answered when he understood her, and an aunt who overheard him nodded and said:

"Anita sends her love, and she will meet you in Paris. She is old and cannot travel."

Serena, in a happy stupor, smiled and smiled.

The countess watched her from the doorway.

"She has no conception," she whispered to the princess. "Had *you* any idea of this?"

"I am almost an old woman," replied the princess sadly. "You may guess that I have ceased to be exclusive about my admirers. It is said that one can count a woman's age by her lovers, and that when she is content with young Argentines, she may be anything over fifty. But at sixty one never knows by whom one may be rejected."

"The mother is not here," said Flor.

"No," replied the princess. "And that is ominous."

"Well," said the countess, a little uneasily, "it is a great thing to be married."

But the princess had passed the age of cruelty, and, watching Serena, she made no reply.

They went in to dinner. The countess had abdicated the position of honour, and Martin drew out the bride's chair. On her right sat Count Montague, on her left his chief uncle, a grizzled old gentleman from Nicaragua. There was a chattering of reedy voices as the relations tried to group themselves in order of their importance, for both the countess and Martin had been too busy to attempt the arrangement of the table. Serena, silent with happiness, and awed by so much brilliance, looked round her new family. Of what disappointment had Martin hinted? Why had her marriage for a moment been in question? She

looked at the countess, who nodded back
at her encouragement which failed to
encourage; she looked at Martin; he
would not meet her eye. What had he
meant, her icy friend? Was this not good
enough for her who yesterday had nothing? This Portuguese clan, these precious stones, these lustrous, friendly eyes,
this gathering in her honour, the heavenly
formality of the wedding eve? And
Martin had said she was a "catch." She
laughed at the thought, and looked
gratefully at the deliverer beside her, and
her fingers stole to the pearls at her
throat.

To be honoured and cherished, when
she had been poor and despised, to be surrounded by a new family, when she had
had none but herself to aid her, to be
respected, to be *married* to Montague!
Martin was mad. He must be for ever
meddling, he could not let happiness rock
itself to sleep.

Hardly had the first course been served
than there was a stir in the hall. A lifted

voice was heard bubbling, lilting, sweet, exotic.

"Anita!" groaned the old gentleman on Serena's left, to Montague on her right.

"Anita has come after all," whispered the guests, aghast.

"Is it your mother, Montague?" cried Serena, delighted, but her fiancé was staring at the door.

Martin bent over the countess.

"I have put Mrs. D'Costa in the boudoir, Madame," he murmured.

The countess rose and left the room. Conversation was palsied and full of whispers. The moments passed, and while the princess continued to talk, Serena continued to be silent. The footmen laid down the plates for the fish and Martin took up the silver tray of lobsters.

The door opened and the countess returned. Smiling slightly she resumed her empty chair between the two young men who had risen on either side of her.

"My child," she said smoothly to Serena, "go and make friends with your mother-in-law. She wants to see you before she joins us."

Serena rose, the eyes of the party on her. In the hall she paused a moment and hoped for Martin. But Martin apparently had no advice for such occasions and remained in the dining-room.

Serena laid her hand on the boudoir door and opened it softly.

The lady who waited within the room did not hear the latch of the door, for the window was open on the street and the sounds of London filled her ears. She stood with her back to Serena, hatless with the sheen of a silk shawl flowing from the crown of her head to the bulk of her folded arms.

Then she turned, and Serena, who had no sense of half shades, no sense of class or race, who wisely thought Martin a gentleman, and any guest a lackey, could at least tell black when she saw it.

Drooping, she stood still near the door and the lady moved a pace forward.

"It is too late, too late"—thought Serena wildly.

228

She remembered Martin's laugh, and his pallor, she remembered the set look on the face of the countess. Though she had not known where she was going, nor where the countess was hurrying her, to what false brilliance of marriage, to what fabulous and *déclassé* world, she knew at last that she was marrying the son of a full-blood Indian. "I am to be married to-morrow!"

That evening the countess drank Serena's health, and Martin whispered, "You have done what you could in a tight corner."

And when the evening was over and the guests were in their bedrooms, that night the bride crept down the back stairs with a candle.

"But he is rich," said Martin implacably, and barred her way to the pantry, "and willing to marry you. It is better to be married in Iberia than single in London.

"True he is the illegitimate son of a Nicaraguan Indian woman, by her first lover, a Spanish Creole. True he is not a count at all, and has no name beyond Montague, given him as a joke by his mother's second lover, an Englishman. But it is true too that his mother, though dark, was once a beauty and married an Argentine. Dying, he left his money equally between the mother and the adopted son.

"And if, by some standards, though rich, and willing to marry you, he is not——"

"Yes?" whispered the bride.

"Well, what of that?" said Martin. "I am not quite a gentleman myself."

The bride's hand shook, so that the candle fell from its socket and rolled down the stairs.

"Martin, Martin," she whispered with a sob into the darkness. "There is still time. Won't you marry me yourself?"

But she heard his feet going from her, for to such a proposition Martin did not think it worth while to reply.

On the wedding day the bride's lovely

body was sheathed in white satin, and
with orange blossom in her hair and the
emerald ring strung round her throat,
she was driven to church.

Martin had boomed her with the reporters, and a row of cameras awaited
her on the stone steps.

"Bride or bridegroom?" whispered the
ushers.

And the duke's daughter, slipping in
after the procession, answered "bride,"
and turned to the left.

At the head of the aisle on the left sat
the Countess Flor di Folio. At the head
of the aisle on the right sat a Nicaraguan
Indian.

The bride's side of the church was almost empty. Her poor colleagues and
companions, her rivals, her seducers,
nurses with children and a rabble from
the streets; these came in to see her
married.

The bridegroom's side was a-flutter
with hats umbrageous and feathery,
toques, jewelled in operatic splendour,
the green of the jungle, the scarlet of

parrots, the jests of Worth and the pleasantries of Lanvin.

The great church was full of shadows, and before the altar, with faces hidden from the congregation, stood the motionless forms of the bride and bridegroom.

The organ changed its note. The hush of the congregation broke.

As the bride came down the aisle she was shivering but she was married.

In Martin's face as she passed there shone relief. There had been moments when he had been half afraid he might have to marry her himself.

THE END